D1650039

The End of Everything: Book 5

Christopher Artinian

CHRISTOPHER ARTINIAN

CHRISTOPHER ARTINIAN

DEDICATION

To those we leave behind.

CHRISTOPHER ARTINIAN

ACKNOWLEDGEMENTS

Tina is not just my wife, my business partner, my publicist, my PR woman…she is my everything. Thank you for everything you do.

As always, a huge thank you to the gang across in the fan club on Facebook. I could not ask for a better group to hang out with. They keep me smiling, they keep me going and their support, loyalty and friendship leaves me in a state of bewildered awe. Thanks guys.

Thank you to my editor, Sheila, and thanks to my mate Christian; your covers never let me down.

And finally, a massive thank you to you for purchasing this book. Even after twelve books, I still get the same feeling of nervousness and excitement. It never goes away and thank you for buying this book and being a part of it. I will never take this feeling for granted.

1

Wren hit the door with the end of her javelin three times before stepping back. She felt her sister's presence by her side as they both looked towards it. After a few seconds, she tried the handle, and the door swung inwards. She tapped on the frame again, but nothing greeted them. "Seems empty," she said, turning around to look at the others.

A sudden crash made Wren and Robyn spin back around. The hallway remained clear, but now they could hear thundering feet.

"Where the hell are they?" Robyn cried.

The guards backed away from the door, leaving the two sisters standing there with their weapons raised. They saw dancing shadows against the hallway wall as a family emerged from a room at the rear, a mother, father and two children: the perfect zombie family unit.

Robyn fired an arrow. As it disappeared into the dimly lit interior, Georgie and Stevenson came to stand by her side. They had their rifles raised, ready, in case the first line of defence fell. The arrow lodged in the father's skull, but all four figures continued to charge towards daylight.

"What the h—"

"Get back," Georgie said, interrupting Robyn.

"Stuff that," Robyn replied, drawing another arrow and firing immediately. This time, the mother creature flew backwards, but the two younger beasts and the father were still hurtling towards them.

"Ughhh!" Wren grunted as the javelin left her hand and shot down the hallway like a guided missile. It smashed through one of the children's chests and continued, burrowing itself into the father's stomach. Both figures crashed backwards onto the floor.

Robyn and Wren were deaf to the fevered growls, but the rest of the group did not have their experience, and the nervous tension in the air was palpable. As the other infected child loomed ever closer, Robyn sensed Georgie's impulse to use her gun. "No," she hissed, knowing only too well what turmoil could unfold if there were more creatures in the vicinity. She drew another arrow and fired. The creature dove at the same instant, and before anyone else could react, Wren lunged from her crouched throwing position, just as the arrow whizzed by. Her shoulder smashed against the younger creature's body as it flew through the open doorway. The sound of multiple rifles being brought up sent a shudder of panic through Wren. The last thing she wanted was for one of these idiots to accidentally shoot her.

Wren reached for her knife as she and the beast somersaulted to a crashing stop on the pavement. The two creatures in the hallway writhed and rolled, causing the javelin to come free and topple onto the carpet. Now, pounding feet began to drum down the hallway once more.

Robyn immediately fired another arrow, causing the younger beast to drop like a sack of bricks. The father creature, still with the shaft sticking out of its head, charged, and now she did hear its growls as it desperately reached through the shadowy confines of the hallway towards the light, towards fresh prey, towards her. She nocked another arrow and fired; this time it plunged into the beast's forehead and the well-built figure crumpled, skidding across the remainder of the carpet and coming to a shuddering stop on the doorstep.

Robyn loaded the bow again and swept around to aim towards the beast that Wren had tackled. For a moment, they were tangled in a blurry fracas, but then Wren parried the creature's arms with her forearm, sending it off-balance. There was another blur as she thrust her knife through the monster's temple. As it stumbled, its face smashed hard against the pavement, and just like that, it was all over. Wren stayed there for a moment, doubled over, catching her breath. She looked at Robyn and Robyn looked at her.

"You okay?" Robyn asked. Wren just nodded. "How the hell didn't that first one go down when I scored a headshot?"

"It happens," Wren said, still trying to catch her breath. "Actual living people have bullets to the head, nails through the head, all sorts. It was bound to happen sooner or later."

Georgie walked up to the doorway to look inside then banged on the frame. No further sound or movement came from within. She turned to look at the guards. "Okay, you know the drill," she said, gesturing for the guards to head into the house.

The men paused momentarily, looking towards the creatures then towards each other before gripping their rifles tight and heading in.

"I want a raise," Wren said through heavy breaths.

"You two are something else," Georgie replied, looking down at the slain creatures. "You're both okay?"

"Oh yeah, we're just peachy," Robyn said.

"Go get yourselves a drink; I think you deserve it."

The two sisters walked across to the armoured minibus. The engine was still idling, as was the engine of the 7.5-tonne truck parked behind. Two guards stood beside each vehicle, their eyes searching the surrounding streets and gardens for any sign of movement.

"Impressive," a good-looking young guard called Dan said as the two girls joined them.

"If you thought that was impressive, you should see me on the dance floor," Robyn said with a twinkle in her eye. Dan smiled and handed both of the girls a bottle of water.

"This is crazy," one of the guards said. He was a man in his early twenties with a pale complexion and frightened blue eyes. "There's no reason for us to be out here."

"I tell you what, Priscilla, you stay at home and help out with the laundry next time so you don't have to worry about breaking your nails," Dan replied, causing two other guards to laugh.

"Get stuffed. All I mean is we're out here, taking this risk, when we've got cellars full of food and we're growing more all the time. Where's the logic in us risking our necks like this?"

Dan was about to respond when Wren butted in. "Listen, it's only a matter of time before someone else comes through here doing what we're doing. Yes, we've got supplies and yes, we're growing more food, but Georgie and Stevenson are thinking ahead. All it needs is one bad winter, one bad harvest, and our stockpile will start to dwindle. We've got over two hundred and fifty people over at the Manor. The more we prepare for the worst to happen, the better we'll be able to manage when it does."

The young guard looked at her and his face flushed with embarrassment before he turned once more to survey the rest of the street.

"Here we go," said one of the others, bringing his rifle up. Two creatures had appeared at the top of the street and were now sprinting towards the group.

"We've got this," Robyn said, raising her bow. "No point in making noise if we don't have to." She fired an arrow and nocked a second. She was about to fire that too when she heard the strum of a smaller bowstring and caught sight of a blurred object sailing towards the second beast. Both creatures hit the ground with thuds. Wren and Robyn stayed in position for a moment, waiting to see if any other monsters were lurking. When they were sure the coast was clear, they relaxed and went to retrieve their respective missiles. They both looked towards the pale-faced guard whose rifle was noticeably shaking before looking towards each other.

"It's like being out here with a bunch of school children," Wren whispered as the two of them walked up the street.

"You're the one who keeps telling me to give them time; try to be considerate."

"I know but...come on...there's a limit."

"A couple of them really keep complaining. Yesterday one of them said that Cromore would never expect them to do this kind of crap. I think there's trouble stirring," Robyn said.

They reached the bodies of their two victims. Wren retrieved the bolt, wiping it clean on the dead creature's shirt before placing it in her case, and Robyn did the same with her arrow. She put it back in the quiver, all the time looking up and down the street.

"I wouldn't worry. It's not like a single one of them have got a backbone. They were happy to go along with whatever Cromore said. They'll be happy to go along with whatever Georgie and Stevenson say...just as long as they don't have to make any decisions themselves."

"I hope you're—" Robyn spotted more movement. It had been an old woman in life, a frail figure in a blood-stained, pale pastel green nightgown with lacy frills at the bottom and around the arms. It dragged its left foot; its body had not been capable of running for some years by the look of it. Wren turned towards the beast. Its arms reached out desperately. It was twenty metres away at least, but its head did not seem to compute distance as its fingers pinched together, hoping to grab onto one of the girls.

The sisters just watched. This was a monster, yes; its pallid and wrinkled skin, the growl, although shallow and quiet compared to most, was still there, still echoing the malevolent sentiments that continued to drive the creature forward. It was a grey day, dark for this time of year, and the beast's pitch-black pupils were like coins devouring the two girls long before the creature's mouth would ever get a chance. It continued towards them, but as it got closer still, Robyn and Wren saw the beast had no teeth.

In all the time they had been on the road, they had never seen anything so pathetic. "That's so sad," Wren said.

"Scary, isn't it? Another fifty years and this could be you."

"Stop it."

"I mean, granted, she's got better hair, but—"

"I said stop it, Bobbi. It's not funny, it's horrible. Don't you ever wonder what lives they had? I mean, she was someone's mother, someone's gran. She'll have had loved ones. She'd have had a life. She might have been someone important, and now..."

"We can't think like that. You can't think about the people they were, otherwise, it will drive you mad." Robyn brought up her bow and fired. The creature collapsed to the floor instantly. "If you start thinking that way you might start hesitating. And out here, that's not something any of us can afford to do."

Wren let out a sigh. "I suppose you're right, but it doesn't make it any less sad."

They stood in silence for the next few minutes, guarding the top of the street, occasionally looking back down to where the guards were standing. Eventually, the team that had gone into the houses began to file out with bags and boxes. They loaded them into the van, and Robyn and Wren took one last look around before going to join them.

"I think that should do us for today; the truck's more or less full," Georgie said, handing Wren her javelin back as two men spray-painted red crosses on the doors to signify the houses had been checked for anything useful.

Robyn and Wren climbed back into the minibus and they were on their way back to what was now their home. "Are you okay?" Wren asked as she saw Georgie holding her stomach.

"Yeah, just stretched my stitches a bit, I think."

"I've told you before—you should be resting up, not going out on scavenger missions. There are plenty of us."

"Yes Mum," she replied.

Stevenson and Robyn smiled. "Go on, make fun of me. I'm only trying to help."

Georgie leaned across and placed a hand over Wren's. "I know you are; you're sweet. I'll be fine, thank you."

It was the third street in Aberfeldy they had cleared in as many days. Most of the town had turned; the only remaining survivors from the population of fifteen hundred or so who hadn't fled when the initial outbreak started were now residents at the Manor. The minibus turned out of the street and immediately sped up as another beast came charging towards them. The smoke plumes from two huge fires had lured the zombies out of Aberfeldy, but there was still the odd one here and there.

The minibus had metal panels bolted and welded to its frame, and attached to the front was a zombie plough: an arrow-shaped wedged that smashed anything in its path. The creature in the road continued to run towards them until they heard a muffled thud. The tyres bounced as they ran over the broken body and everyone in the bus conjured a visual image of the aftermath. The vehicle carried on for another hundred metres and then came to a stop.

"What's going on?" Stevenson asked.

"Caravan!" the driver said.

"Sweet," Stevenson replied, as Dan opened the back doors and the group climbed out once more. Robyn and Wren raised their bows while the rest of the guards brought their rifles up, panning from side to side checking for movement.

The driver climbed out of the minibus as well and led Stevenson back a few metres. He pointed up a driveway that continued straight past a dirty red brick semi-detached house. Peeking out from the rear garden was a tow hitch and the front panelling of a four-berth caravan.

"Nice spot," Georgie said, walking up behind them. "The car's still in the garage, I'm guessing the house might be occupied."

"Yeah," Stevenson replied. "We should probably clear it while we're here." He looked back towards Wren and Robyn. "Girls!"

The two sisters looked at each other before Wren returned to the minibus to collect her javelin. The whole unit operated like a well-oiled machine now. Robyn went to stand at one side of the front door and Wren at the other. Georgie, Stevenson and the rest of the guards all stood in a semicircle with their rifles raised towards the entrance. Wren tapped on the door with the end of the javelin and they all waited. She repeated the action, they waited for a few more seconds, and when nothing came, she tried the handle while Robyn stood back with her bow raised, covering the entrance.

"Locked," Wren said.

Stevenson looked towards one of the guards, who pulled a long crowbar from his backpack. Robyn and Wren stood ready. They were the first line of defence. They could kill the predators with virtually no noise; if the rifles needed to be used then things had really turned bad.

An eardrum bursting crack echoed up the street as the door and frame separated. Suddenly everyone's attention was no longer on the door. Now, their eyes were darting in every direction, afraid that any creatures in the area would be making a beeline for them, but after a minute, when nothing appeared, their heart rates returned to normal. The guard returned to the door and shouldered it in, displacing a few more wood fragments. He paused in the entrance, looking in for a moment before stepping over the threshold. "Phwoar…something stinks in here."

Wren, Robyn and the rest of them followed him into the living room, and as the door opened, the smell of rot became overpowering. "I think I'm going to puke," said the pale guard who had been complaining earlier on.

"Oh god!" Georgie said, bringing her hand up to her mouth. A man was sitting in an armchair, cradling a little girl who had been no more than eight or nine. The girl had a chunk bitten out of her neck and someone had put her to rest before she transformed, as her alabaster skin had not turned to the familiar grey of the creatures. Closer inspection revealed a screwdriver protruding from the base of the little girl's skull. There was an empty pill bottle on the coffee table, and the woman who sat in the chair opposite stank of whisky, as the remains of her glass had spilt down her front. The scene told a dismal story.

Everyone stood in silence, looking from one chair to the other. Wren stared at the suitcases and holdalls that had been piled by the side of the door in the open plan dining room. "This was us," she said under her breath.

All heads turned towards her, but it was Robyn who spoke. "How do you mean?"

"Look," she said, pointing over towards the door. "They were getting ready to leave. They were going to head somewhere safe and then the little girl got bitten, just like Dad got bitten. They had plans to find safety as a family, then it all came crashing down around them in an instant."

The rest of the group looked towards the suitcases, then back at the dead family. "It's heartbreaking is what it is," Georgie said.

"Come on," Stevenson said, let's get this done and get out of here."

Robyn, Wren, Georgie and Stevenson walked through the open plan living room and into the kitchen.

There were three boxes of food on the countertop by the back door. "Looks like our job has already been done for us," Georgie said.

Wren picked up a small dish full of keys and started looking through them. "I think this is the one for the caravan," she said, unlocking the back door and stepping out. She opened the caravan door and stepped inside with Robyn close behind her.

"I could totally have this as my pad," Robyn said.

"We've got a place," Wren replied.

"Yeah, but this could be my chick cave," she said with a smile. "I mean, look at it…TV with built-in DVD player, nice big fold-out bed, built-in wardrobes, kitchen, gas heater, my own personal bathroom." Robyn looked around the caravan with widening eyes and a widening smile on her face.

"Uh-huh. And are you going to empty the toilet when it's full?" Wren asked.

"What do you mean?"

"What do you think happens when you flush?"

"Erm…I dunno. I've never really thought about it."

"No…really? You surprise me. It all goes into a big drum and then you have to empty it."

"What?" Robyn said, horrified. "I thought it was, like, hooked up to the drains or something."

Wren let out a small laugh. "You really haven't got a clue, have you? It goes into a drum, you empty it, and quite often you'll get big splashes of what comes out over your hands and your clothes, and if you're really unlucky, your face. More often than not it will dribble over the container and then you'll have to wipe that clean as well before you fit it back in the caravan."

"That is so gross. I think I'm going to be sick," Robyn said holding her hand up to her mouth.

"So, do you want me to have a word with Georgie? See if we can still have this as your chick cave?" Wren said, grinning.

"Erm, no…thanks." She looked around the interior of the caravan one last time. "It was a nice dream while it lasted."

They stepped out into the grey afternoon. Stevenson was already at the front of the house-on-wheels and had started lowering the jockey wheel. Once it was safely down on the drive, he tightened it up and swung the caravan around, taking it wide from the house before turning it towards the road and manoeuvring it down the driveway. Two more guards joined him to make sure he did not lose control as he steered it down the incline. When they reached the road, the minibus reversed into position and they hooked the caravan to the tow bar. Four more guards headed down the drive carrying the food boxes and another box of assorted swag.

"Right then. We'd better be heading back," Georgie said, coming out to join Robyn and Wren. "All in all, that's been a pretty good day. We got a van full of food and supplies, a box full of seeds, a flat-pack greenhouse, and we've finished it off with a plush new caravan," she said.

"Yeah," Wren said, looking back to the house. "It wasn't a great day for everyone though, was it?"

Georgie let out a sigh. "We can't think about that. We can't think about all the stuff that's happened to all these people. If we dwell on it, it will kill us."

"So what? We just forget about them all?" Wren asked.

"I'm not saying that," Georgie replied. "I'm just saying…most of the world has gone. People we knew…and…people we loved. Every day we're going to be reminded of it, but we've got to think about what we've got, too. We've got to think about building something. We're here…my daughter's here. I have to make sure there's a life worth living for her, otherwise, what's the point?"

The three women just stood there in the drive for a few moments longer as they watched the final preparations to get the journey underway once more.

"Why don't we—" Robyn stopped talking as soon as she started.

"Why don't we what?" Georgie asked.

"Never mind. It's stupid," she replied.

"Go on, Bobbi, why don't we what?" Wren asked.

"Why don't we have a remembrance?" Robyn said, a little embarrassed. "So we can think about all those we lost. We could have a day...each year...like a day of the dead. To remember all of them."

"That's a beautiful idea," Georgie said.

"That would be lovely," Wren said.

"We'll do that, Robyn. We'll have a day of the dead," Georgie said, smiling. She took hold of Robyn's hand and gave it a gentle squeeze before heading down the driveway to the waiting vehicles.

"You're not just humouring me?" Robyn asked.

"No," Wren replied. "I think it's a great idea." The two sisters smiled at each other and headed towards the vehicles. They came to the road and Robyn carried on, but Wren stopped abruptly. Georgie was holding the back door of the minibus open for Robyn and she cast a glance to the pavement to see why Wren had stopped moving.

"What's wrong?" she asked.

Robyn turned around to look towards her sister. "Wren, what is it?"

Wren did not answer. Her eyes were still looking down the road in the direction they had come from. She had seen something, but for the time being, her brain could not register what exactly.

Wren began to walk, very slowly, at first, down the road. "Wren? Wren?" Georgie said, letting go of the door. She and Robyn both shot each other concerned looks. "Wren, what is it?" Georgie asked again.

"I saw something," she replied distantly.

Robyn and Georgie went to join her. "What? What did you see?" Robyn asked.

"I'm not sure."

"Okay, so why are you freaking us out?" Robyn asked.

"There!" Georgie said. "I saw it."

"Oh great, another one," Robyn replied. "Saw what exactly?"

"I think it was someone ducking behind a hedge," Georgie said.

"There!" Wren said, pointing.

"I can't see a thing," Robyn replied, getting increasingly frustrated.

"What should we do?" Wren asked.

"We should go to them. Find out if they need help," Georgie replied.

"Hey! Newsflash! If they're ducking behind hedges to avoid being seen by us, chances are they're not interested in making contact. Let's just get into the bus and head back home."

Suddenly the figure stood up straight and disappeared between two houses. Georgie and Wren both looked at each other then both started sprinting down the street.

"Oh god," Robyn said under her breath before heading after them. When they arrived at the spot where they had seen the figure, all three of them searched the gardens, the garages, the two houses, but there was no sign of anyone.

Georgie walked up to the hedge where she had seen the figure duck. She looked around, but it was only when the smell of cigarette smoke entered her nostrils that she looked to the ground. There were two stubs in the grass. She picked up both; they were hot to the touch.

"No sign of anything," Wren said as she and Robyn joined Georgie.

Georgie held the two cigarette stubs up. "I wouldn't say that," she said. "There were two of them, and judging by the impressions on the lawn they were here a while...watching us."

"Why would somebody just stand here watching us? Why wouldn't they just run if they were afraid?" Robyn asked.

"That my friend, is the million-dollar question."

2

A crowd gathered around the minibus and the truck as it always did when they returned from a scavenger mission. The gates were kept closed at the Manor all day long, so it was always an event when they were opened. A group of armed guards always used to encircle the entrance, and everyone present held their breath until the gates were closed firmly once again.

The second Georgie stepped out of the minibus, her daughter, Pippa, ran up to greet her. Because she had experienced pain with her wound earlier, she refrained from picking the little girl up, but instead knelt down and threw both her arms around her, squeezing her daughter with everything she had.

"Missed you, Mummy."

"Missed you too darling, but I'm back now," she said, standing and taking Pippa by the hand as she walked across to see her mother and father.

Almost immediately, the shutter on the back of the truck was raised and the day's treasures started to get unloaded.

"Everybody!" Georgie called, immediately gaining the attention of all present. "We're going to have a meeting in the dining hall tonight at eight o'clock. Please can you get word around to everyone?"

Those assembled looked at each other, wondering what the meeting could possibly be about, but all muttered in the affirmative with regards to spreading the word.

One of the older-looking guards immediately walked up to Stevenson to give him a report of what had been going on in his absence. A group of men and women emerged from entrance doors with sack carts, the wheels bouncing from one step down to the next before reaching the back of the van where they loaded up with all the booty.

Robyn and Wren were about to head inside when Georgie called them over. "Robyn, I'd like you to tell everybody your idea tonight."

"What? No, I….You should talk to them. People listen to you."

Georgie laughed, as did her mother and father, "You've got to be kidding me. I don't think there are two people here who command more respect than you and Wren. You could tell people the moon was a giant meringue and they'd believe you."

"I'd rather not," Robyn said.

"You should," Wren said, "it was a really good idea."

"Look, go get yourselves a bite to eat and meet us in the dining room at eight. If you feel up to it, fine, if you don't, I'll do it. But it is a great idea, and it should come from you," Georgie said.

"Okay, see you at eight," Robyn said, heading up the steps and into the Manor.

"You wouldn't think she'd be nervous, considering how gobby she normally is, would you?" Wren said.

"Have a word with her. It should come from her," Georgie said.

"I'll do my best, but don't hold your breath," Wren replied, climbing up the stairs and following her sister.

She walked through the doors and immediately heard banging and construction work as she went down the corridor to their apartment. The ceiling that had collapsed when they had made their escape was now almost fully repaired; another week or so and the whole place would be restored to its former glory, physically, anyway. What happened on that fateful day would stain the walls of this place forever.

Robyn opened the door to their apartment and went straight to the kitchen cupboards. She pulled out a box of Pop-Tarts and immediately started munching. "Want one?" she asked as crumbs flew out of her mouth.

"I was going to make us a sandwich," Wren replied.

"What with?"

"Erm...bread...duh!"

"I mean with what in it?"

"Honey."

"Huhey?" Robyn replied, her mouth so full of stodgy material that she could barely move her lips.

"Yeah!" Wren said, smiling and pulling out a jar from her rucksack. "They brought Mrs Tatum's hives across yesterday. They've got them round the back. I forgot to tell you—she gave me a jar before we left this morning."

Robyn took it from her sister and unscrewed the top, placing what was left of her Pop-Tart down on the kitchen surface. She unscrewed the lid and immediately stuck her finger in, withdrawing it with a big glob of thick, yellow goodness stuck to the end. "Sweet," she said, swallowing what remained of the Pop-Tart and sticking her finger in her mouth.

"It's like watching Winnie the Pooh after he's had every last ounce of self-control surgically removed. I've got to eat that as well, y'know! You can't just stick your dirty fingers in."

"It's so good," Robyn said, ignoring Wren's protestations.

"You are so gross. I'd say you were like a pig, but pigs have way more etiquette."

Robyn peered into the jar and was about to get another dollop when she glanced across to the Pop-Tart she had put down on the countertop. She looked back at the jar and her eyes lit up with excitement. "I have just had like...the best idea ever." She reached into the cutlery drawer and pulled out a knife. Without pause, she dipped it in the honey, swapped the jar for the Pop-Tart from the counter, and spread the thick honey all over the pastry.

Wren just stood there, her mouth gaping. "Erm...heart disease anyone? That is so unhealthy."

"Yeah, but it tastes so good though," Robyn said, smiling.

"It's like you literally have no processes in between thinking something and doing it. Bacteria ponder decisions longer than you do," Wren said, pulling half a loaf from the bread bin and cutting herself a slice.

"Yeah well…" Robyn screwed up her face and broke wind loudly. "Ponder that," she said before taking another bite of her snack.

"Ughh! I cannot believe we're related sometimes."

"Tell me about it," Robyn replied, only with the mouthful of food she had, it sounded like, "te me baht ih."

Wren shook her head, finished making her sandwich, and went to sit down in the other room to eat it in peace. After a few minutes, Robyn joined her. She sat back in an armchair and crossed her hands over her stomach. "Full now?" Wren asked, taking the last bite from her sandwich and placing the plate down carefully on the coffee table.

"I could do with a nap," Robyn said, closing her eyes.

"How could you possibly sleep with so much sugar in you? I'm surprised you're not bouncing off the walls."

"You're the science geek. Don't ask me how my body works."

"Anyway, you can't sleep. You need to figure out what you're going to say at the meeting."

"Stuff that," Robyn replied, straightening up in her chair. "There's no way I'm getting up in front of all those people."

"You did it before."

"Yeah, that was different."

"Not really, Bobbi. That was about throwing people a lifeline, making them realise that we could survive together. This is just as important. This will give people a chance to mourn what they've lost. We talked about this when we were back at the farm. We never got the chance to do it properly. I doubt anyone has. We've got two-hundred and fifty people within these walls, all very different, all very scared, all trying to find out where they belong in this new world. Honouring our dead is something that will bring everybody together...make them realise that we all have something in common."

Robyn let out a sigh. "Okay, I'll do it, but you're coming up there with me. I'm not facing this crowd all by myself."

"That's fair enough; I can live with that."

*

The dining room was full when Robyn and Wren walked in at five minutes to eight. The long, sturdy table had been positioned at the front of the room and nerves began to jangle in Robyn's stomach as Georgie led her and Wren down to the front.

Georgie stepped onto a chair and then onto the table and the conversations that were bristling around the room came to a hush. She glanced towards the entrance and Stevenson took one more look up and down the outside hallway before nodding to her.

"Okay, thank you, everybody, for coming. This won't be a long meeting. When we were out today, Robyn came up with a really great idea, and I wanted her to share it with you." Georgie looked down towards the two sisters and beckoned them onto the makeshift stage before she climbed down.

Wren stood a little behind her sister. She leaned into her, "You'll be great. Just relax."

Robyn looked around at all the expectant faces and the butterflies began to flap faster in her stomach. "Well...it's not...erm...I just thought...erm."

Robyn's anxiety was palpable, and Wren stepped forward to stand with her sister shoulder to shoulder. "It's funny, back at home we could never shut her up, and now we can't even get her to start."

A wave of laughter went around the room, and for a moment, Robyn went bright red, but then she laughed a little, too. She looked at Wren and smiled. "Well...I...I was just saying. An awful lot has happened in a very short time. I don't think any of us have had time to digest it. I know I haven't...we haven't," she said, glancing aside towards her sister before looking back over the audience. "We watched our dad become one of those things. We watched our mum get bitten. We never got to lay them to rest...properly, I mean. We've pretty much been on the road since all this began. We've all lost friends, we've all lost family, all over the country...all over the world." Robyn paused and looked around the room to see people were hanging on her every word.

"Go on, you're doing great," Wren whispered.

"So, anyway, I thought we should have, like, a day of remembrance, a day of the dead. I remember watching a thing on YouTube once about how Mexicans have a holiday to remember the ones they've lost. I think that would be a nice thing to do...for all of us...for all of us to come together and remember those, not just our families, but everyone." Robyn looked around as the audience stood in stony silence. "Er...that's it, really. That's what Georgie wanted me to say." She looked down towards her friend, desperately hoping she would rejoin them on stage, but for the time being, she remained still.

"I think that's a beautiful idea," said a woman in her thirties from the middle of the crowd.

"Great idea," called out a man.

"Could we have a service?" asked another.

Robyn looked from face to face, not sure how to respond to any of them, and now Georgie did climb back onto the stage.

"Okay, we can sort out all the details later, but I just wanted to find out if people liked the idea. Can we have a show of hands for?" Every hand in the room shot up, so many, it was impossible to see if someone had not raised theirs. "Maybe it would be easier if we asked to see those against," she said, but not a single hand rose.

A woman at the front looked around, then looked towards the stage. "I'm guessing that's a yes, then," she said, smiling.

Georgie clapped her hands together. "Right then. Well, unless anyone has objections, we can do this a week on Sunday. I'll set out a suggestion box, and people can put in their thoughts about what they'd like to see or do. Now, before everybody goes, I just wanted to give you a little update regarding the scavenger missions."

"You haven't found me a Bentley yet, then?" asked an old man near the front, and everyone chuckled.

"No, Angus, we haven't found you a Bentley yet. Now, as you'll be well aware, we're going out every day to gather supplies. If there is something that you're needing, put a note of it in the box by the main entrance. We can't promise anything, but if we can find what you're after, we'll bring it back. Please be sensible; we can't be carting around life-sized glass sculptures or sixty-inch TVs. The main purpose of these missions is to bolster our food, agriculture, fuel and armament stocks. Mr Cromore's library full of first editions, although beautiful and valuable, isn't of a huge amount of practical use to us at the moment so we're restocking that as well. We're collecting books on farming, on medicine, on building. We're searching out textbooks because we've got a couple of teachers here and we're wanting to start classes for the children. We're also gathering building supplies, plumbing supplies, electrical supplies."

"Why?" asked a voice. "We've got water, we've got power, we've got—"

"Granted, those of us who live in the Manor have it, but the people in the caravans, the trailers, the makeshift homes on the grounds don't. We have plans to hook them up too. We want this place to work for everyone. We want everyone to have the same benefits and the same chances as everyone else. We want this to be a proper community where we can all work for the benefit of each other, so it's very important that the families who are living in the grounds get to enjoy what we have, too," Georgie said, looking around at all the nodding heads. "We have every chance to make this place work. That means looking out for each other, doing the right thing and supporting each other. I'll be damned if we have an US-AND-THEM thing here like there was before. It's just going to be an US thing."

"Yes!" shouted out a voice as some people started to clap.

"And if someone's not happy, if someone thinks they're getting a raw deal, I don't want to hear disgruntled murmurs; I want to hear it out loud so we can deal with it and get it sorted," she said, looking towards a group of guards at the back of the room.

Nearly everybody began to clap and cheer. A smile lit up Georgie's face, until her eyes settled on Susan, near the doorway. Susan was not clapping, she just stood there looking around the dining room at all the happy, cheering people. She cast an icy glare towards Georgie before turning around to leave.

When the excited crowd had finally dispersed and gone back to settle into whichever corner of the Manor grounds they now called home, Georgie, Wren and Robyn remained in the dining room, sitting on the table that, a few minutes before, had been their stage. "You both did really well," Wren said.

"It was Robyn who was the real star. She got them all going," Georgie replied.

"Did you see the death stare from Susan?" Robyn asked.

"You saw that too, did you?" said Georgie.

"It was hard to miss," Wren replied.

"Has she said anything to either of you two lately? I know you were pals."

"Pals might be stretching it a bit," Robyn replied. "She hasn't really had much to do with us since it all happened. That afternoon when she drove us to the mill, she was pretty odd then, and to be honest, I can't remember one proper conversation I've had with her since, but I have noticed she's been...weird. Weirder."

"We need to keep an eye on her," Wren said.

"What do you mean?" Georgie asked.

"We killed her mum and dad and we took her house. She might be planning something."

"You're worrying over nothing. Susan's not like that. But I guess she has been acting strange," Robyn said.

"Yeah...just like her mum did."

3

Fry put his feet up on the thick wood of the function room table. He leaned back in his chair and stared at the man who was talking to him. TJ remained at the bar for a moment, sensing the change in atmosphere. He prepared three Glenmorangies and placed them carefully on the serving tray. He had sustained a fracture to his left arm in the car accident, and the Loch Uig doctor had insisted on him resting it and keeping it in a sling for a while until it healed properly.

He always did what the doctor ordered. That guy creeped him out more than he would ever let on. He had been struck off and imprisoned over twenty years ago for abusing some of his young and vulnerable patients. He'd served time, and when he got out, he went to work for gangsters, patching up wounds that they couldn't go to regular hospitals with. He earned more there than he ever did as a GP. He was a lowlife, like most of the population in Loch Uig, and TJ had dealt with plenty of lowlifes. But Doctor Penning sent inexplicable shivers through him.

TJ picked up the tray in his right hand, made sure it was well balanced, then proceeded across to the table. He put it down, served Fry his drink, passed one to the other man, and kept the third for himself. He took his seat next to the big, fiery-haired Glaswegian, and sat back, waiting patiently for the eruption.

Fry picked up the glass of amber liquid and examined it for a moment, watching it slosh around in the crystal tumbler. "So, what you're telling me is you saw a well-organised, well-armed group empty a house. One squad went into the house while another guarded the road. They loaded up a truck and had an armoured minibus, and they scored themselves a caravan, too. And when they'd finished, they just drove off."

"Yeah," the man said, taking a drink of his whisky. "Anything else?"

"Nope. They just got back into their vehicles and drove away...oh, but before they did, one guy walked up to the door and spray-painted a big red cross on it."

Fry stared long and hard at the man again before climbing to his feet. He picked up his whisky and took a drink. "And where did they go, exactly?"

"No idea, boss," the man said, shrugging his shoulders, not willing to tell Fry for a second that he'd been spotted, or that the group hadn't just driven off, as he'd said.

"No idea boss," Fry repeated.

"And why don't you have an idea?"

"Well...like I say, they just drove off. We were in this garden y'see and—"

Fry banged his palm down on the table, making TJ and the other man jump. "I swear, the sooner your arm heals, the better, because if I have to deal with these bumbling retards any longer, I'm going to start killing people, and when I start, I swear on my mother's grave, I won't be able to stop. Sort. This. Now!" Fry downed the rest of his drink in one, slammed the glass down on the table then stormed out of the room.

When the door closed with a boom behind him, TJ took another drink of his whisky and looked across at the man. "You'd better find these people."

"How? They could be anywhere."

"Rollins, use your brain for once in your life. Why do you think they painted a red cross on the door?" Rollins shrugged. TJ let out a sigh and took another drink. "They painted a cross on the door to show that they'd been to the house. If you went around town you'd find more crosses."

"So how's that going to help us find them?"

TJ's shoulders sagged and he drained his glass. "If they want to mark what houses they've already searched, that means they intend to come back to search more. So…?" TJ gestured for Rollins to finish his thought.

"So we go back there and wait and when we see 'em, we grab 'em."

"No! For god's…. Look. If these guys are well-armed, we don't want to get in a firefight with them. If you blow them all away, we're not going to find anything out. We need to be smart, stealthy. You saw which road they headed out on, so get some look-outs positioned along it, along the branches of it. I bet over the course of a few days, we can figure out exactly where this lot are from. They could be sitting on a wee goldmine, and the last thing we want is for their defences to go up."

Rollins nodded, "Okay…I understand…but I still think we could take a couple of them and get answers…the girls at least."

"So they've got women going out with them too; that's a good sign. Means they must be short of real men."

"No, not women, actual girls. We saw a couple, and they looked like they were straight out of school."

TJ put his glass down and glared towards the other man. "What?"

"Yeah, they were with this older-looking bird. All of them looked like they'd be popular attractions in the Fun House," Rollins said with a leery grin.

"The girls, describe them."

"Well, one had shortish black hair, carried a bow…black leather trousers, leather jacket—"

"And the other one?"

"Blondish hair tied back in a ponytail, very trim, tight jeans. She had some kind of spear."

"Blonde with a ponytail? What was her face like...her eyes?"

"She was a bit too far away, but I wouldn't have said no."

TJ straightened up in his chair. "Listen to me...listen to what I've told you...do not engage with these people at all. I don't care if they firebomb you, just get in your cars and drive away. We need to find out where their base is. Don't screw it up, Rollins, otherwise Fry will be the last of your worries."

The smile suddenly left Rollins' face. He was used to Fry's ill-temper, but he had never seen such venom in TJ's glare. "Sure, of course! You know I wouldn't let you down." He looked at his glass and thought about taking another drink, but instead, he got to his feet. "We'll head out first thing tomorrow. However long it takes, we'll find them, TJ, I promise you."

TJ said nothing, he just fixed him with a stare. His mind was racing as he watched Rollins leave the room. Could it be the same girl? When he had heard that Aberfeldy was empty, he assumed right then that he would never get a chance to lay his hands on her, but now...what were the chances of a similar looking girl, clearly a risk-taker, showing up?

TJ remained by himself in the function room for several minutes after Rollins had left. He was a practical man, not like Fry. TJ was all about business, the task at hand...so why did this feel different? Those men he lost, the vehicles he lost, the time he lost, the injuries...they were just the cost of doing business. So why did he want revenge so badly? He wanted to find that girl and make her suffer like he had never made anyone else suffer. He thought back to that pursuit...he thought back to the second he knew his vehicles was about to crash...he thought back to that look in the girl's eyes. He would never forget them, and if he got the chance, the vengeance in his eyes would be the last thing she ever saw.

*

They had set off earlier than usual, and the occupants of the minibus were lost in their thoughts as it weaved through the woodland. "Where are we going again?" Robyn asked wearily.

"A farm," Georgie replied.

"Farms are ten-a-penny around here," Wren said.

"This one's a bit different," Georgie replied.

"Different how?"

"It's one of the big ones. It's not some ma and pa outfit. It's owned by a huge conglomerate. A fleet of wagons, machinery…but most importantly, it's got its own fuel pumps. We've got more jerrycans and containers than you can count and we're going to stock up, hopefully, with enough fuel to keep us going for months."

"Is it far?" Wren asked.

"About three miles on the other side of Aberfeldy."

"So how come we're going so early?" Robyn asked grumpily.

"Well, that way we can make the fuel run, head back to the Manor, drop it all off, and still have time to hit a few places in Aberfeldy itself."

"So we get to work a double shift? Super."

"You have to forgive my sister. Her mornings used to start in the afternoon, and even then it sometimes required specialist equipment to separate her from the mattress," Wren said.

"Well, if you prefer, after we've done this run, I can bring along one of the other guards and you can have a break. It has been pretty non-stop for you girls since—"

"We're fine," Wren said. "Ignore her. I know it's hard sometimes, but trust me, over time you can gradually tune her out."

The minibus sped through the streets of Aberfeldy. The occupants knew there were still a few creatures here and there, so they stayed alert, peering down alleyways and into gardens. They were through the small town and on the other side almost within the blink of an eye.

The houses and streets gave way to country lanes and fields, and after a few more minutes, the minibus slowed and turned onto a wide track. A little further on, Wren could see imposing, corrugated steel barns and other sturdy buildings. She reached into the rucksack by her feet and withdrew her two crossbows.

"Hopefully we're not going to need those," Georgie said.

"Hopefully," Wren replied, "but I'd rather have them and not need them than need them and not have them."

Georgie smiled. "Every day I understand a little better how you two survived out there by yourselves."

"How did you find out about this place?" Wren asked

"Everybody knows about this place, but a couple of the men from Cromore worked here. They were the ones who told us about the fuel."

The minibus came to a stop in a huge, open yard between two massive corrugated steel constructions that looked more like aircraft hangars than farm buildings. The driver pulled on the handbrake. "Well, we're here," he said.

"No shit, Sherlock," Robyn mumbled.

Everybody dismounted from the back of the minibus, but the truck behind them kept its engine running. "They said the tank was off to the side of one of the buildings," Georgie said.

"Over here!" shouted one of the guards.

They all walked around the corner, keeping their eyes peeled just in case. There were two diesel pumps standing back to back.

"How do we get the fuel out with no power for the pumps?" Wren asked.

"We don't get it from the pumps," one of the guards replied, "we get it from the main tank...the one that the fuel truck pumps into," he said, walking around the back of the larger vehicle and opening the doors. He climbed up as the rest of the guards assembled to collect the empty containers. One of them grabbed a manual pump and a long reel of hose. The yard became a flurry of activity while Robyn and Wren took their positions. Georgie joined them. She had her rifle strapped around her shoulder but had also borrowed Wren's javelin.

"Don't you think you should have sat this one out and let Stevenson come instead?" Wren asked.

"I need to be seen to be doing more...to be prepared to do more than anyone else. People are watching me. Everything me and Stevenson do, and if they think for a second we're going to sit back and let other people take the risks, that's when dissent will start, and once it starts, it's like a downward spiral. We need to breed positivity; proactivity will keep spirits up. We want every small win to seem a huge victory," Georgie said, as if she'd rehearsed the lines in the mirror a thousand times.

"Oh my god…it's like listening to an older version of my sister," Robyn said.

"You've woken up then," Wren smiled.

"Nobody should be out of bed at this time."

"Well you shouldn't be so damn good with that bow, then you wouldn't be in as much demand," Georgie said, grinning.

"Georgie!" called the guard who had removed the cover from the main fuel tank.

Georgie let out a sigh. "What now?" she muttered under her breath as she walked across.

"We're too late," the guard said as she came up beside him.

"What do you mean we're too late?"

"Someone's beaten us to it?"

"What?"

"It's empty."

"But there must have been, like, hundreds of gallons in there," Georgie replied.

"Try thousands, but that doesn't change the fact that there's not a drop in there now."

"Oh crap!"

4

The guard carefully screwed the stopper back on the tank before replacing the cover. The dismay in the air was palpable and threatened to erupt into panic, and Robyn and Wren gave each other a concerned look.

"Okay...okay...we can salvage something here. The vehicles...there must be hundreds of gallons just sitting in the tanks. Let's get into the—"

The side door to the nearest steel superstructure burst open and two of the guards appeared. "Same story in there," one of them said to the man by the fuel tank cover, not even noticing that Georgie had come across to join them.

"It can't be!" Georgie said.

"There's a big gap where a few of the trucks had been parked, and the rest of them are all empty," the guard said. "Every single tank. Whoever came here, they took their time, it seems. They were pretty thorough, I'll give them that."

"But...but...the resources you'd need to do this...the manpower," Georgie said.

The guard who had replaced the cover stood up. "Makes you think, doesn't it," he said looking at Georgie.

"This makes it all the more important that we get what we can while we can," she said. "Are there any other places around here, Strand?" she looked towards the guard who had checked the fuel tank.

"There's McClintock's place, just on this side of Aberfeldy. It's tiny in comparison to this, but if nobody's been there, there should be some red diesel kicking about, at least to keep the tractors going."

"Okay," Georgie said, "let's see if we can salvage something from this at least. Load up."

Within a few minutes, the minibus and the truck were rolling again. There was an uneasiness prickling the atmosphere, and everybody's eyes peered through the small slits in the armoured sidings to watch for anything out of place as they navigated the roads.

"I say we should forget about these bloody trips. We've got enough to feed the five thousand down in those cellars; we're getting crops from the polytunnels already and it won't be long before the rest of the crops start coming through. I say we should close those gates and keep them closed, keep our heads down. Hopefully, if we don't bother anybody, nobody will bother us."

"Spoken like a true hero, Cadmore," Georgie replied bitterly.

"He's right," said another of the guards. "What's the point of taking risks?"

"You as well, Birmingham? You think we should just lock ourselves away and hide from the outside world?" Georgie asked.

"We can control what goes on in there; we can't control what happens out here," Birmingham replied.

"Oh, yeah. And when winter comes and we need meds, how well do you think we'll be able to control things then?" Georgie asked.

"We've got meds," replied Cadmore.

"We've not got enough for two-hundred and fifty people, not by a long way. We've not got enough soap, sanitary products, cleaning agents, replacement parts for the vehicles, materials to patch the polytunnels up with if we get a storm...there is so much we haven't got that we haven't even thought about and—"

"Yeah, so if a vehicle breaks down, we go out and find the parts; if a polytunnel gets damaged we find something to patch it up. If—"

"Listen to yourself, Cadmore. By the time we need stuff it will all be gone, that's why we need to move now. That's why we—"

"Georgie's right," interrupted Robyn. "There's a time that I would have thought like you, but then I figured out what was going on out here. You think keeping your head low will help if the wrong people find you? Cos let me tell you, it won't. If they find you, you have two choices: you fight or you run. Trust me on this."

"Yeah, and if you hide away, frightened of what you might face, then you may as well put up the white flag straight away," Wren added.

Cadmore and Birmingham both looked at each other and sat back, not wanting to engage in conversation any further. Even in the dim light of the minibus, Wren could see a smirk appear on Georgie's face. They travelled the rest of the way to the farm in silence. When the driver finally pulled on the handbrake, Cadmore and Birmingham were the first to exit the vehicle. As the light rushed in, Wren and Robyn could both still see Georgie's self-satisfied smile, and they couldn't help but smile too. They stepped out into the open with the rest of the guards, and as the truck parked behind them, they could tell right away that something was amiss. The farmhouse door was slightly ajar, and the hairs on the back of Wren's and Robyn's necks bristled. They brought their weapons up, and the rest of the guards, finally noticing what they had noticed, brought their rifles up too.

Georgie slowly advanced towards the farmhouse door with the sisters at either side of her. The others hung back for a while before reluctantly following.

"Stay behind me, girls," she said, raising the rifle.

"Erm, actually, if those things are around, I think it makes more sense for us to go first, don't you?" Wren said, placing a hand on Georgie's arm.

Robyn and Wren sped up towards the door. They paused outside before Wren nudged it open with her foot and ducked down, immediately pointing her crossbows into the kitchen. Robyn stood with her back straight, panning the bow from side to side, checking every nook for movement. There was a trail of blood over the terracotta tiles leading through the kitchen and into the house. Wren looked towards her sister, who nodded, and the pair edged into the house, Wren remaining low, Robyn keeping the bowstring taut and her arrow nocked.

They advanced further into the property and were about to head down the dark hallway when there was a thud behind them. Both girls spun around, Wren's fingers pressing a little harder against the triggers, Robyn's fingers flexing a little more against the string. Their hearts jumped in that instant, both of them expecting the worst, expecting the scene they had witnessed so many times before.

"It's me, it's me!" whispered Georgie, putting one of her hands up.

Wren and Robyn both gave her vexed looks as they turned back around and followed the trail of blood. They headed down the hallway and stopped again as the trail led into a bedroom. The door was closed, and Wren ducked down, placing one of the crossbows on the floor and putting her free hand on the doorknob. "You ready?" she whispered.

"Yep."

Wren twisted the knob and flung the door open. Robyn was about to fire when she stopped and brought the bow back down. There was a figure sitting in a chair. If he had ever been a danger, that time had passed. Blood covered nearly all of his torso. There were two clear bullet entry wounds in his vest, and the colour had left his skin, but not like it left the skin of the creatures. This poor man had simply lost too much blood. Whoever had shot him must have left him for dead and somehow, he had dragged himself out of the kitchen, down the hall and onto that chair. His hand had fallen by his side, the girls could see it was gripping onto something. Wren picked up her second crossbow and placed it in her rucksack before heading over to him.

She pulled up his hand. "It's a picture." She looked at it more closely. "I think it's his family."

"Oh god, the poor man," Georgie said, joining Robyn in the doorway.

"It looks like his wife and two daughters in the picture with him," Wren said sadly.

"We'd better spread out and look for them," Georgie said.

"Don't waste your time," Robyn said.

"What do you mean?"

Robyn and Wren looked at each other, but it was Wren who spoke this time. "I think we know these people. I think these are the ones we ran into before."

"What?" Georgie asked.

"When they looted the house that we were staying in…it didn't stop there. They left men behind to wait for us. They were going to take us…back with them," Wren said.

"Take you?"

"I think they take the women as prizes."

Georgie's face went pale. "Oh Jesus."

"Yeah," Robyn said as she and Georgie stepped further into the bedroom. "You can tear this place apart, but I don't think you're going to find anybody else, and I'm guessing you're not going to find any fuel either."

"Listen…you can't tell the others about this. You can't say that stuff—it will cause panic. We'll just say that the wife and daughters must have escaped while he put up a fight. If word of this got around the Manor, it would be disastrous."

"Erm...Susan already knows," Wren said.

"Oh god," Georgie replied, slumping onto the bed.

"I mean, the good thing is that she's not really talking to anyone…other than herself?"

"Oh Christ! What happened?" asked one of the guards, looking at the gruesome figure in the chair.

"Looters, we're guessing. Looks like his wife and girls managed to escape though, otherwise there'd be a sign of them somewhere," Wren said.

"Poor bastard," said the guard. "Well look, this place is like the other, bone dry. Whoever came here left with everything worth having."

Georgie just sat there for a moment weighing all her options. Eventually, she let out a breath and stood up. "Okay, let's head out. It's still early; I'm determined this isn't going to be a wasted day."

"Head out where?" asked the guard.

"We haven't even scraped the surface in Aberfeldy, let's get back there. We'll do this the hard way. There are plenty of cars and vans in that town, and there must be a lot of diesel and unleaded sitting in those thanks, so we'll siphon them," Georgie said.

She walked past Wren, Robyn, and the guard and headed back out to the waiting vehicles. Within a few moments they were back on the road and the mood was even more sombre than before. The guard had gone into detail about what he'd seen, and, subsequently, painted a grim picture for the others that hung in the minibus like a black rain cloud.

"This is stupid," Cadmore said. "We know these people are well organised, we know they're armed and we know there are loads of them. But we're still staying out here. I say we put this to a vote. Who wants to head back to the Manor?" He and Strand both put their hands up.

"We're not putting this to a vote!" Georgie said firmly. "Look, if you want to behave like a couple of timid little schoolgirls—"

"Screw you!" Strand said. "You've got no right—"

"I've got every right. We're trying to build something back at—"

"Build something?" Strand interrupted. "We had something before, but you and your lover-boy tore it all down."

The bus was travelling at some speed, but it did not stop Georgie from climbing out of her seat and reaching diagonally forward to grab hold of Strand's collar. "You never speak about John. Do you hear me? You are not man enough to so much as utter his name."

Cadmore, who was sitting next to Strand, grabbed hold of her wrist and yanked it hard, but didn't manage to pull it free. "He's right, you stupid bitch!" Cadmore shouted. "Cromore had all this sussed out. We were much better off under him than we are now." Cadmore swept his arm around in an attempt to bat Georgie away. He didn't make contact, but she ducked back and lost her grip on Strand.

The minibus went around a bend, and the driver, who was so preoccupied with the unfolding drama, as were the other occupants of the minibus, nearly lost control. Georgie had to grab hold of two headrests to brace herself, and Wren leaned forward, placing a steadying hand on her back. As soon as the bus was on a smoother course, Strand was out of his seat, bowing his head to make sure it did not bang on the ceiling of the minibus as it travelled. He had both of Georgie's wrists in his hands. "You know I'm speaking the truth," he shouted in her face.

"We were all better off under Cromore," Cadmore shouted, turning in his seat and looking towards the faces of the other men as they watched the scene playing out in the dim light of the minibus interior.

"You were all slaves, hired hands, mercenaries. All Cromore wanted was power. All he wanted—"

"I'd rather be a well-fed mercenary than this!" Strand shouted.

"Let go of her," Wren demanded, but Strand just cast her an icy glance before looking back towards Georgie, whose face was now contorted with fury.

"What's the difference between us and them? They're looters; what do you think we're doing? The difference is, they've got a bigger bloody army by the sound of it, and I bet they're not interested in building some fairytale utopia. They'll be—"

"I said let go of her," Wren said again.

"Keep your mouth shut, little girl. It wasn't until you two turned up that everything turned to crap anyway," Cadmore shouted.

Georgie, her wrists still tightly clenched in Strand's fists, looked around at the other faces to try and gauge the feeling, to confirm that the only person intervening was a fifteen-year-old girl.

"I say we head straight back to the Manor. We tell the people what's going on and we have a leadership vote. I don't ever remember anyone voting you into power," Strand spat.

"I said, let go of her now!" Wren stood up and aimed both her crossbows towards Strand.

"Wren, no!" Georgie said.

"You'd better put those down right now, little girl or today is going to be a really bad day for you," Strand said.

"I'm not going to tell you again," Wren said. "Stop the bus."

"You wouldn't dare," Strand said, looking towards the two crossbows.

"If you don't let go of Georgie, you're going to find out, aren't you?"

It was too confined in the minibus for Robyn to use her bow, but as the vehicle came to a halt, she reached down and picked up the javelin, ready for action if things turned bad…to worse.

Strand maintained his clutch on Georgie's wrists and looked around at the others. "Who's with us? Who's for heading back to the Manor and changing the way things are done around here? We were all better off under Cromore and there's no reason it can't go back to—"

The sound of the crossbow string twanging was almost perfectly synchronised with the howl of pain that came from Strand's mouth. He immediately let go of Georgie's wrists, his right arm dropping limply by his side while his left hand shot up to the bolt that had torn through the fleshy part of his right arm near the bicep.

Georgie paused momentarily until what had happened sunk in, then she unleashed a hammer blow to Strand's face. The sound of the crack was like a gunshot in the confined space, and everyone looked on in shock, Cadmore most of all. There was an explosion of red as cartilage and soft tissue spread, and so stunned was Cadmore by the eruption of violence, that it was not until he tasted his friend's blood in his gaping mouth that he fully realised what had happened. Strand staggered, then fell in the narrow aisle. Cadmore just watched on a moment longer before scrambling to help his comrade, whose face and shirt were now painted dark red. And just like that, the mutiny was over.

Cadmore managed to drag Strand to his feet and get him settled back in his seat, albeit dazed and confused. Without prompting, the driver set the wheels in motion once again. Georgie grabbed hold of a headrest to steady herself from the initial jerking motion, then she went back to her seat and sat down. Her eyes were wide, and she kept looking down at her fist, horrified, almost as if she was looking at someone else's gory knuckles.

"Are you okay?" Robyn asked.

For a moment Georgie didn't answer; she just kept moving her hand around, looking at Strand's blood trickling between her knuckles and down to her wrist. It wasn't until Wren put a gentle hand on her shoulder that she looked up. "Are you okay Georgie?" Wren whispered.

"No," she replied. "No, I'm not."

5

The remainder of the journey into Aberfeldy was almost silent. When they had set out that morning, nobody could have anticipated such events, and there was not a soul, including the participants of the drama, who was not shaken by them.

When the minibus came to a stop, one street along from the houses they had raided the previous day, all the occupants dismounted, apart from Cadmore and Strand. There was a strong coppery smell in the back of the vehicle which slowly began to dissipate as fresh air rushed in. The wound had not bled as much as Strand had expected, but there was still a fair-sized crimson stain on his shirt.

"Strand," Georgie said, "come here into the light so I can take a look at your arm. I'll see if I can get that bolt out and get it bandaged up."

"Screw you," came the muffled reply.

Georgie stood there a moment longer, cast another look into the bus, and then said, "At least let me give you some painkillers."

"I said leave me alone. I don't want your help."

"Suit yourself," she replied, leaving the two men on the bus and going to join the others.

One of the men was already briefing the occupants of the truck about the drama that had unfolded, and Georgie knew that she was going to be the subject of lots of gossip and hushed whispers over the coming days and probably weeks; she hoped that would be the extent of the community's reprisal. While the rest of the men pulled containers and pipes out of the back of the truck, ready to siphon what they could from the vehicles parked in the streets, Georgie ushered Wren and Robyn to one side.

"You girls really are something else. You know that, don't you?"

"They're idiots and you're our friend," Wren said.

"But you realise, you're in it up to your necks with me now. These guys aren't going to be happy, and if something comes to visit me, they're going to lump you two in with it as well."

"And?" Robyn said.

"All I'm saying is that you've opened up a whole lot of trouble for yourselves."

"You seriously think we're scared of a couple of prissy little whiners like that? Ooh…'things were so good before,' and 'I never had to do this, we never had to do that…' Winging little shites. See how they like being stuck on top of a van with a hundred zombies trying to tip it over so they can take a bite out of you. They think they know what fear is? They wouldn't last a minute out there," Robyn said.

Georgie laughed. "Thank you. I mean it."

"Like I said, you're our friend. Friends stick together."

Georgie smiled warmly. "John was always a good judge of character. He liked you two from the outset; it's easy to see why."

"Yeah," Robyn replied, "we're just so damn lovable."

They managed to siphon a lot more fuel than Georgie thought they would from the cars in the street, and once that had been loaded into the truck it was back to the routine of going house to house. The familiar tension as the group surrounded a door, waiting, expecting the worst when the door swung inwards made them forget the ugly scenes that had occurred in the back of the minibus.

"Okay," Georgie said, "last one, then we'll take a break."

The first five houses had all been clear. It was like the street had been abandoned. Wren tapped on the wooden door with the end of her javelin and almost instantly there was the sound of hammering. Robyn looked towards her. "Sounds like two at least," she said. "Be careful."

Wren pushed down on the handle, but the door was locked. She looked towards Georgie, who in turn looked at one of the guards. He pulled the heavy black crowbar from his backpack and walked to the entrance. The guard rammed the narrow edge of the crowbar hard against the wood of the door where it met the jamb.

A few splinters of wood fragmented before he removed it and rammed it into the same spot a second time. The frantic battering against the door increased and he looked back nervously to make sure everyone had their weapons raised so if these monsters broke free, they would be put down quickly. More wood splintered from both the door and frame before he pulled the bar free once more.

He could feel his heart beating faster and faster as he thrust the crowbar into the gap he had created. He felt the end scrape against the solid frame as he pulled. There was a crack that snapped through the morning air like a firework, and for the briefest second, the door swung inwards before the pounding creatures on the other side, not possessing the basic intelligence needed to just lever the handle towards them, pushed it back, and continued to beat their fists against the wood.

The job was done now, though, and the man returned to the ranks alongside the others. The beads of sweat on his forehead and running down his back were visible to everyone, but he didn't care. He had done his bit, and next time, it was somebody else's job.

Wren looked towards Robyn and Robyn looked back, widening her eyes and shaking her head almost as if she could see what was going through her younger sister's mind. Before she got the chance to say no, Wren ran towards the door and booted it. There was a thud as it smashed against the creatures behind it, but her action had the desired effect. The door bounced off them, knocking them onto the hallway carpet before it returned to the jamb, only to rebound. It creaked inwards slowly, revealing two beasts scrambling over one another to climb back to their feet. The winner raced towards the opening and gasps could be heard over the sound of the beast's voracious growls as it appeared in the open with the speed of a greyhound. Robyn fired immediately and the beast flew back into the darker recesses of the hall, while its compatriot made a beeline towards Wren.

Wren stood there, waiting, knowing how important it was not to strike too soon or too late. The dancing black pupils of the creature almost disappeared, becoming pinpricks as the sun appeared from behind a cloud, and that was the moment. She thrust the javelin upwards. The point plunged into the monster's gaping mouth, through its pallet, and through its skull. It stopped dead in its tracks, pausing momentarily before crumpling to the ground. Wren whipped the javelin back out as quickly as she had forced it in. She wiped the gruesome residue off on the monster's stained and ragged clothing and let out a breath.

"Clear," Wren said with a smile.

"That was mental. Never do that again."

"Got the job done."

"Yeah, and a thousand different things could have happened as well."

"Yes, Mum."

"Okay," Georgie said, clapping her hands. "We all know what we're doing, let's get it done." The guards shouldered their rifles and headed into the house. "Y'know, I'm with your sister on this one," she said, looking towards Wren.

"Look, I did what needed to be done. End of story."

"Wren, you're very brave, and you're very strong, and that's why you can't afford to take risks. This is bigger than you, than Robyn, than me. When I talk about trying to build something, I'm dead serious, and we need you. We need Robyn; we can't afford for anything to happen to either of you." Georgie put a comforting hand on Wren's shoulder before disappearing into the house after the guards.

"Things are going to get bad, y'know," Robyn said, looking to make sure the two guards who were on street duty were far enough out of earshot.

"What's going to get bad?"

"Because of what happened in the minibus. It's going to cause a lot of problems. Cadmore and Strand aren't going to let this rest. They're going to stir up a load of trouble," Robyn said.

"They're cowards," Wren replied."

"I agree, but what happened is going have repercussions."

"Whoa. I know it's serious if you start using words like 'repercussions.' You didn't bang your head or something when the minibus was going around those bends, did you?"

"Laugh it up, brainiac. We shot one of those guys. They're pissed off and they'll be out to cause trouble—that's all I'm saying."

"I wasn't going to stand by and let—"

"You did good, I'm just saying be careful."

"Okay, okay."

They remained silent, looking up and down the street for movement as was second nature to them now, until, eventually, the scavenger team began to file out of the house carrying boxes, bags and various other items of booty. They loaded them into the back of the waiting truck. When it was all in, Georgie took a cooler from the truck's footwell and placed it down on the road. "Dig in, guys," she said, pulling two bottles and two snack bars out. "I suppose I'd better go and see how Strand and Cadmore are doing."

"Oh yeah, like they would if it was you," Robyn said.

Georgie gave her a small smile, then headed to the back of the minibus.

"Hey guys!" she called. "Anyone seen Cadmore or Strand?"

Two of the guards stopped in mid gulp while another two immediately put their bottles and snacks down to go join Georgie at the bus.

"Cadmore! Strand!" shouted one of the men.

"Erm, given where we are, it's probably not a good idea to start shouting," Georgie said.

The man suddenly looked embarrassed, understanding the stupidity of his actions. The others continued looking up and down the street. They even revisited the houses they had already raided for supplies.

"Their rifles have gone…and their backpacks," Wren said, climbing out of the minibus. "Good riddance I say."

"We can't just leave them out here," one of the men said. "Don't get me wrong, I think Cadmore's a wimp and Strand's a right tosser sometimes, but leaving them here would be a death sentence."

"We've got a few more houses to check. They know where we are. If they want to leave, there's not a lot we can do," Georgie replied. The group continued to look around for a while and then slowly moved towards the cooler once again. They grabbed their drinks and snacks, all the time keeping one eye on the street, expecting to see Cadmore or Strand come around the corner...but it never happened.

*

"My bloody arm," Strand said, clutching his wound once again.

"We should find somewhere to stop, haul up for a little bit, see if we can get that bolt out," Cadmore said.

"I'm open to suggestions," Strand said, looking up and down the street. "You fancy knocking on one of these doors to find out if there's anyone in?"

"Maybe if we can get out of the town, find a farmhouse or something, maybe—"

"Neither of you move another step!" called a voice, and both men stopped dead in their tracks. "Drop your weapons and put your hands up!"

Cadmore threw his weapon on the ground before the voice had finished talking, but Strand had a little more difficulty. He slid the rifle from his shoulder and it clunked heavily onto the tarmac. He raised one hand, but the pain in his other arm was so excruciating, he couldn't manage to lift it.

"I can't raise this hand. I've been shot," he shouted.

Six men suddenly appeared—three from behind one garden hedgerow, three from another. All of them had raised rifles trained on the two men. "Shot, you say?" one of them called.

"Yeah. Crossbow bolt," Strand said nodding down to his arm.

"Sounds painful."

"You've no idea."

The man walked forward, his weapon still raised. He looked at the rifles laying on the ground. "Where are you from? Who else is with you?" he said, looking behind them.

"Nobody's with us," Strand said.

"Lying isn't a good way to make new friends," the man replied.

"Look," Strand said, gesturing towards his arm, "would you stick around with people who did this to you? We came here with others, we're heading out on our own...at least we were."

"Why did they shoot you?"

"Because I spoke the truth."

"The truth can be a dangerous business," the man replied.

Strand looked at the weapons the six men were holding. They all carried sidearms, too. "I'm guessing we're not going to be heading off by ourselves after all," Strand said.

"Please!" said Cadmore. "Don't hurt us. Take our guns, take our stuff, just let us go."

"Don't panic, friend," the man said, waving his arm for the others to lower their weapons.

Strand raised his eyebrows in surprise. He had assumed a bullet would be making its way towards him any second, but now he relaxed as much as a man could relax with a crossbow bolt in his arm. "So we're free to go?" he asked.

"What's the rush?"

"We want to get out of this town, get to a place where I can get this damned bolt out of my arm, and figure out what we're going to do next."

"What were you doing here anyway?" the man asked.

Strand let out a sigh, but it was Cadmore who spoke. "We didn't want to be. We said it was a bad idea, but that bitch won't be happy until everybody's dead. Power-mad, she is."

"Slow down," the man said.

Strand gave Cadmore an irritated look, but Cadmore's eyes were firmly on the man asking the questions. "There's this place, it's a few miles down the road, and we were all set there. We could have weathered out anything. It was this guy, a landowner who set us up...food, water, supplies. He trained us," Cadmore said pointing down towards the guns. And we were growing food, getting along great, then it all went to hell."

The man looked at Cadmore and then at his own men. "And you wanted things back to the way they were? The sensible way...the safe way," he said.

"Yeah...that's right."

"What if I told you there was a place like that? What if I told you there was a place where people were safe and nobody went hungry and they all had an equal share of the spoils? What if I told you there was a place where every man banded together and stood by each other's side and fought for each other? A place that had a pub, and a gym, and plenty of soldiers to make sure everyone was safe. What would you say if I told you that?"

"I'd say how do we get there?" Cadmore replied with a smile on his face.

The man smiled. "All you'd need to do is come with us. I think you two will fit right in."

"Seriously? You'll take us?" Cadmore asked.

The man reached for the radio receiver on his belt. "Bring the vehicles, we're on the road that runs parallel to the cenotaph," he said, hitting the talk button. Less than a minute later, two army Land Rovers pulled up. "Come on lads, I can't wait to introduce you to the boss."

Two of the men walked towards Cadmore and Strand, they picked up the rifles and the backpacks then headed towards one of the waiting vehicles. Cadmore started walking towards the man who was beckoning him to climb into the car; he shot a glance back to Strand, who was just standing there.

Strand looked behind him down the street, then back towards the waiting vehicles. "What have you done, Cadmore?" he said under his breath.

6

A heavy atmosphere lingered in the minibus like a chilling mist as they headed back to the Manor. There had been arguments and disquiet before, but they had never had two people desert them.

"Look," Dan said, turning to the rest of the group. "We all know Cadmore and Strand wanted the easy life. They both would have been quite happy to carry on with the way things were, but they weren't willing to put their lives on the line for anything...I mean, seriously...if you were in a firefight, how happy would you be if one of them had to cover your back?" He turned back in his seat and the rest of the short journey was silent.

The minibus pulled up outside the gates, and they slowly swung open as the watch guard signalled the all-clear. On one of the missions, they had procured a set of wheeled safety steps from a warehouse. The resident builder had managed to attach brackets to it which fixed it to the wall, so it wouldn't topple if they had high winds. He waved them in with a smile.

Cadmore and Strand would not really be missed by anyone, but the effect of arriving back with fewer people than they set off with would cause a stir.

Stevenson was the first to greet Georgie as she climbed down from the minibus, and she was about to take him to one side and brief him when her parents and Pippa rushed towards her with welcoming smiles. "I'll speak to you in a minute," she said to Stevenson. "We've got a problem." She took Pippa's hand and walked to one side while the crowd continued to gather around the vehicles.

Robyn and Wren were greeted with warm nods and smiles as they moved through the crowd. They started heading up the steps, looking forward to getting back to their apartment, when Stevenson caught up with them. "What happened?" he asked.

"I'm sure Georgie will—"

"I'm asking you, Wren. What happened?"

"There was trouble. Cadmore and Strand."

"What? Were they...was it the zombies?"

"No. They…"

"They've always been troublemakers," Dan said. He had been listening in a few feet away. "They got out of hand. Strand was trying to start a revolution. He had hold of Georgie, Wren fired her crossbow and he took one in the arm. Him and Cadmore stayed in the bus while the rest of us cleared the houses. Next thing we know, they'd gone. Cleared out with all their stuff."

"And the other men? How did they react?" Stevenson asked.

"They didn't," Robyn said. "They stayed silent."

"What do you think, Dan?" Stevenson asked.

"About what?"

"Does this have the makings of a bigger problem?"

"I…"

"You're forgetting to mention something, aren't you?" Wren interrupted.

"There's more?" Stevenson asked.

"That farm...the big one you wanted us to go to. The farmer had been shot. All the fuel...everything had been taken. That's what started it all. There's somebody out there;

they've got a lot of resources and they're not too fussed about trampling on anyone who gets in their way," Wren said.

"This just keeps getting better and better," Stevenson said.

"From the look on your face, I'm guessing you've been given the good news," Georgie said, joining the four of them.

"Turned out to be some trip. Remind me never to let you go without me again," Stevenson said with a thin smile.

"We need to talk," Georgie said.

"I thought we were."

"I mean inside."

"Okay, give us a few minutes to make sure—"

"I can take care of all this," Dan said. "It's just a case of getting stuff logged and down to the cellars. It's not rocket science."

"Okay, mate. Thanks," Stevenson replied.

"Come on," Georgie said, "we'll go to Wren and Robyn's place; it's nice and private there."

"I suppose that's my afternoon nap gone out the window," Robyn said.

"It's good you can make jokes. We're going to need all the smiles we can get soon," Georgie replied.

"Who was joking?"

*

The journey to Loch Uig took less time than Strand expected, which he was eternally grateful for. He knew he was a lamb heading to the slaughter, and could feel little but despair as Cadmore was completely taken in by his new "friends."

The man who had done all the talking back in Aberfeldy had introduced himself as Rollins, and as he turned to look at them now with his wide, friendly grin, all Strand could see were shark's teeth in his mouth; all Cadmore could see was the key to a sweeter life.

"We should be there pretty soon. I'll introduce you to my boss, TJ. We can give you a tour of the place, and if you like it, you can stay. If you don't, then you can take your rifles, your backpacks, and we'll even give you a few supplies for the road. No hard feelings."

Cadmore grinned, "That sounds brilliant. From what you've told us already it sounds like just what we're looking for, doesn't it?" he said turning to Strand.

Strand faked a smile. "Sounds great."

The fields gave way to woodland and eventually, the road became sandwiched between tall cliffs on either side. Rockfall netting covered them, suggesting landslides had been a frequent issue in the past, and all Strand could hope for as he looked out of the side window was the netting would break, the car would stop, and he would have the chance to make an escape. But it was not to be.

Rollins turned in his seat once again. "We'll get our doctor to take a look at your arm, as well."

"Doctor?" Strand asked.

"Hell yeah! We've got an all-singing, all-dancing medical centre. Even got nurses in uniform, haven't we lads?" Rollins said, laughing and coaxing laughter from the other men, who had remained quiet up until now.

The Land Rover slowed down as it approached a barricade. On top of the barricade stood four armed men. Rollins signalled to them, and one of them disappeared as a thick, wooden gate covered by a patchwork of metal sheets and offcuts slowly opened, allowing the two vehicles entry.

Like a small child, Cadmore looked on in wonder, his head turning to watch the gate get pushed closed again as they travelled through. "You weren't kidding when you said 'safe,' were you," Cadmore marvelled.

"You haven't seen the half of it yet. I can guarantee, there is no place like Loch Uig on the planet."

Suddenly Strand's heart sank a little further.

*

"Pop-Tart?" Robyn asked, offering Georgie and Stevenson one of the pastries from the open box in her hand. They both declined, so she grabbed one for herself, took a huge bite, and placed the box back down on the countertop. The kettle was boiling and Wren had already put teabags in the four mugs. When the tea was brewed, they adjourned to the living room. Wren and Robyn flopped down onto the couch while Georgie and Stevenson took an armchair each.

"So, it was a well organised, well equipped, and pretty brutal armed gang…" Stevenson said looking towards Georgie before turning his head towards Wren and Robyn, "…and you think it's the guys you've run into before?"

"It's a coincidence if it isn't them," Wren replied.

"True. Let's hope it is them," Stevenson replied.

"Why would you wish for that?" Wren asked horrified.

"Because if it isn't, that means there are two outfits like this operating."

"I suppose that's a fair point."

"Look, it doesn't matter who it is, all that matters is what we're going to do about it," Georgie said. "I think we should downplay this thing. I think we should keep the scavenger trips close to home for now, and if we see more evidence of these guys operating in this area, then we should regroup and rethink."

"That's probably wise, although we should take a look at the map and see where else we might be able to source a decent fuel supply," Stevenson said.

"What about the mill where we got the lorries?" Georgie asked.

"Chances are the roads around that area will be swimming with the zombies after Banksy lured them with that fire," Stevenson replied.

His words hit Georgie like a freight train. When she kept herself busy, she could bury the pain of losing John deep inside, but the raw feelings of loss always stabbed her when somebody mentioned him. She took a drink of tea to mask the start of a sob. "Erm...yeah, I forgot about that. But there must be—"

"I think that's mad," Wren said. "I don't think we should play this down. I think we should prepare."

Robyn swallowed and took a big slurp of tea. "Have you met my sister, Joan of Arc? She won't be happy until she's martyred herself and everybody she knows."

"Wow, Bobbi, another correct historical reference. Did you find a fact a day calendar or something that you haven't told me about?"

"Har-di-har!" Robyn said, taking another bite of her Pop-Tart.

"When they show up, we should have this place like a fortress. We should have everybody trained. We should have—"

"Slow down," Georgie said, "What makes you so sure these people will show up?"

"This isn't just a band of thugs we're talking about. They're organised; methodical. We've seen and heard them in operation. I know what you're thinking...that I'm just a girl, and I've got a big imagination, and—"

"Nobody thinks that at all," Georgie said. "You and Robyn command more respect around here than anyone."

"Then listen to me...please."

"We are listening, Wren, but—"

"But nothing. What have we got? A handful of guards with guns. There are plenty of guns and other weapons down in the cellar. Let's arm everyone who can carry a weapon. For the ones who are no good with guns, we'll give them spears...give them slingshots, for all I care, just give them something. If those men come here, let's give them a proper fight. We can build defences, we can build all sorts. The longer we let the rumours circulate about what's going on out there, the worse it's going to be. I say, tackle this head-on, now."

"What are you, like, forty?" Georgie said, laughing.

Wren folded her arms, "That's right, make fun of me; no wonder you get on so well with Robyn.

"I'm not making fun of you...well...maybe I am a bit, but...you're fifteen and you put better arguments forward than most adults I've ever known."

Wren unfolded her arms. "You mean you agree with me?"

Georgie took a sip of her tea and placed it down on the coffee table. "You make it hard not to," she said, turning to look at Stevenson. "What do you think?"

"I think we're going to have a lot of persuading to do, but yeah, it makes sense. Better we do this sooner rather than later. Are you coming?" he asked Georgie.

"I haven't finished my drink."

"We can drink after. Let's get this done."

The two of them said their goodbyes and left the apartment, slowly heading down the corridor, side by side. "Did you ever think you'd be taking advice from a fifteen-year-old girl?" Georgie asked with a smile on her face.

"Erm, can't really say I did, but then again, I never thought I'd be in the middle of a zombie apocalypse." They walked on a little further. "She seems convinced it's the same group that she and Robyn ran into."

"Whether it is or it isn't, they're not people I want to meet face to face, and we can prepare and drill until the cows come home, but if they show up at our door, we're dead!"

"What's the point then?"

"Hope...hope is the point."

7

Strand and Cadmore sat in the boardroom waiting for the arrival of the mysterious boss that Rollins had told them about. It was the first time they had been alone since getting picked up in Aberfeldy. As promised, Strand was given the attention of the doctor, who removed the bolt from his arm, gave him a shot of antibiotics and a handful of strong painkillers and bandaged him up. Despite being in a little more comfort, his overall mood had not changed.

"You're a moron, y'know that?" Strand said.

The smile of wonderment that had been on Cadmore's face ever since meeting Rollins and the others vanished for a moment. "What do you mean?"

"I mean we're here so they can get information out us about Cromore. Then once we've told them everything they want to know, they're going to finish us off."

Cadmore looked at him for a while, then the smile reappeared on his face. "Naa. You're well off-base. I think if we play fair with them, they'll play fair—"

The function room door opened and a man with his arm in a sling walked in. He joined them at the table and sat down. "I'm TJ," he said. "Rollins said they found you on the street in Aberfeldy?"

"Yeah, that's right," Cadmore replied. "We were going to find a place together and just—"

"A place together?" TJ said, "Erm, so you too are...y'know...more than just mates."

"Jesus no," Strand cut in. "You'll find it's best to avoid prolonged conversation with Cadmore. Words tend to confuse him."

Cadmore looked hurt for a moment, but when TJ let out a small laugh, he smiled too. "So you and these people you were with had a difference of opinion," TJ said gesturing towards Strand's bandaged arm.

"You could say th—"

"That place is a disaster waiting to happen," Cadmore said, gaining TJ's immediate attention. Strand fired an infuriated look in his direction, but it went unnoticed.

"It's this woman running things. We had it sweet. This guy, Cromore, he had everything sussed. Food, water—electricity, even. We were planting crops, so we were going to have a steady supply of food. We had patrols in place stopping poachers and—"

"Sounds like a smart man. What happened?"

"Well this woman and her boyfriend, they killed him and took over. Up to then, we hadn't lost a single person in Cromore, but after, we lost plenty."

"Bit of a bum deal for the rest of the residents," TJ said.

"Yeah, I mean, they're all in the Manor now. They abandoned the village," Cadmore said.

"The Manor?" TJ asked conversationally.

"A big mansion owned by Cromore. It's surrounded by a ten-foot wall and everybody's living inside now. Some in the house, some in caravans, some in lorry trailers, but all inside the walls. The village has gone."

"I see. And this woman," TJ asked, turning to Strand, "she did this to your arm."

"No, it was a little girl," Cadmore said laughing.

"Button it," Strand snapped, and Cadmore stopped laughing as soon as he started. "There are two sisters there. They're good with bows. I was having a disagreement with Georgie, the woman I told you about, and one of them decided to shoot me in the arm."

"A little girl shot you in the arm?" TJ asked puzzled.

"They're not little girls," Strand said, giving Cadmore a dirty look before returning his attention to TJ. "One's fifteen, one's seventeen. They'd travelled with Cromore's daughter, so were welcomed into the place with open arms. They'd been in a few scrapes a bit further south with some zombies and some gangs, so everybody thinks the sun shines out of their arses."

TJ nodded sympathetically. "And they're at this Manor too?"

Strand looked at TJ long and hard before answering. "Yeah...like Cadmore says, everybody's in there."

TJ pulled a large map out of his pocket and unfolded it onto the table. He stood up and leaned over it, pulling out a pencil and tapping lightly against the paper. He looked at Strand and then towards Cadmore. "Whereabouts is this mansion, exactly?"

Cadmore stood up, smiling. He took the pencil and circled the location of the Manor. "Why do you want to know?" he asked.

"Well, it sounds like your pal Cromore was a lot like us. We've got big stores of food, water, fuel and...all sorts. We've got some polytunnels and we've got people digging over veg plots, too. We like to plan ahead and for all the faults of these people you're telling me about, it sounds like we might be able to trade with them. We need to think about the future, now more than ever," TJ said.

"I don't want to go back. I don't want to go back to that place," Cadmore said.

TJ smiled. "Don't worry, you'll never have to. We have trade delegations who do that kind of thing."

"Oh...right...brilliant."

"Well then, let me go find out where Rollins is and he'll give you a tour of the place. I'll see you two a bit later on," TJ said, folding the map back up and placing it in his inside pocket.

When he left the room, Strand turned towards Cadmore. "You're really falling for this hook, line and sinker, aren't you?"

"Falling for what?"

"This act. You honestly think for a second they're going to politely knock on the door and say: hi, we'd like to start trading with you?"

Cadmore looked a little confused. "Yeah, why not? It makes sense."

"You're an idiot. Right now, they're out there figuring out where to bury us, and right after they've done that, they're going to head down to Cromore and finish everyone there off too."

The smile left Cadmore's face again. "So, if you think that, why not try and escape? Make a break for it?"

"Cos there's nothing left. There's nothing left in Cromore, there's nothing left outside, there's nothing left anywhere. We're all just waiting for the end to come. I just hope it comes fast."

*

"TJ told me to give you the full tour. He must like you," Rollins said as they left the hotel.

Strand and Cadmore remained silent for the time being as they walked through the car park. They turned right at the end of the road and immediately saw a big, single-storey building with Fun House spray-painted onto a sign outside the entrance.

"What's that?" Cadmore asked.

"Just what it says," Rollins said. "If you want a bit of fun, then that's the place to go. I tell you what, I'll give you the full tour, and if you both decide to stay, I'll take you there tonight as my guests, how about that?"

"Sweet," Cadmore said. Strand said nothing. His face remained unmoved as he looked further up the street.

They passed a number of men, who all nodded towards Rollins respectfully before carrying on their way. "We're getting new arrivals all the time, but there's plenty of space. We could probably get you a caravan sorted out until we got you something more permanent. Everybody has to pull their weight around here. Everybody has to go out and scavenge, but it's obvious you two are used to that."

"Oh yeah, that's not a problem. That's like old hat to us now, isn't it?" Cadmore said, smiling at Strand.

They reached the top of the street and turned right again. As soon as they did, they could hear music rising into the air. "Now, this here is the local pub," he said, pointing about halfway down. "Don't worry; it's bigger than it looks. Come on, let's go have a drink."

They walked through the doors and a wall of cigarette smoke accosted them. The pub wasn't even half full, but from the noise inside, a blind person could be mistaken for it being packed to the rafters. Rollins led Cadmore and Strand to the bar and a hulking figure with short, black hair and an unkempt beard came to serve them.

"Alright, Rollins. New recruits?" he asked, nodding towards Cadmore and Strand.

"Just showing them around; TJ's orders. Give us three pints, Smurf, will you?"

Smurf stood there and beckoned with his hand for Rollins to hand something over. Rollins reluctantly pulled out a card with a grid printed on it. A number of squares in the grid had already been crossed and initialled, and Smurf crossed another. "And the comp slips?"

"I didn't pick any up."

"Right, well I'll have to put it on your card. You can sort it out with TJ after," he said, crossing and initialling two more squares.

"You're a real piece of work, aren't you? You can see these lads are new; why can't you—"

"What I see doesn't matter. I'm responsible for every drop of booze that flows out of this place and if it's not accounted for I've got to respond to TJ, Fry, and The Don. If you think for a second I'm going to put my nads in a vice just 'cos you can't be arsed to pick up a couple of comp slips then you can go sing," the big man said, glaring at Rollins, who broke out into a smile.

"Okay Smurf, okay…I was just winding you up."

Smurf didn't say another word. He grabbed three pint glasses, filled each of them with draft bitter, and Rollins led the other two men towards the quietest table in the place. When they were settled, they all took gulps from their glasses. Cadmore's grin was wider than ever, but Strand's eyes were scouring every nook and cranny of the pub.

"This place is brilliant," Cadmore said.

Rollins smiled. "The whole town gets a little bit better every day. It's really growing," he said, taking another long drink.

"That man, Smurf, he mentioned two other people…Fry and Don. Who are they?" Strand asked.

"The Don," Rollins laughed. "They're the two big bosses. You don't have to worry about them. They're the brains behind this place; we don't really see them that much. All the orders come down through the lieutenants."

"So how many people are here?" Strand asked.

Rollins took a long hard look at him then had another drink. "Curious type, aren't you? There are enough…hundreds…more than that…any other questions?" he said with a smirk.

Strand sank back in his chair and gave a small shake of his head. "I've got one," Cadmore said. "Why is that big fella called Smurf?"

Rollins laughed. "Oi Smurf!" he shouted over to the bar.

The big man walked across, throwing a tea towel over his shoulder. "What is it? I'm busy," he said, looming over their table.

"Cadmore here wants to know why you're called Smurf."

The big man stared at Rollins, looked towards Cadmore, then let out a sigh. "Few years ago, me and a couple of pals knocked over a security van. One of the bloody cases exploded, covering us all in blue dye. Well, there was a police chase through Milton Keynes centre— made the papers and everything—but it's difficult to blend into the crowd when you're painted blue from head to foot. Anyway, they got us and we got taken in. Took over a week to get all that dye out; needless to say, some smart arse said that I looked like a giant smurf, and the name stuck. There...that's the story...mind if I get back to work now?"

"That's hilarious," Cadmore said.

Smurf just glared at him. "Me getting seven years, hilarious?"

The smile suddenly left Cadmore's face. "Erm, no...I meant…"

Smurf broke out into a wide grin. "Gotcha," he said, as he turned and walked back to the door.

"So, how do you boys fancy coming out with my crew tomorrow?" Rollins said.

"To Aberfeldy?" Strand asked.

"No, it's the other direction tomorrow."

"Yeah, deffo," Cadmore replied.

Strand remained quiet, gave a slight nod of his head and took a drink. Suddenly he realised just how good life was at the Manor.

8

Wren and Robyn walked down the hallway from the servants' quarters. The Manor was unusually quiet, almost as if a giant cone of silence had been lowered over the building. They headed through the empty entrance hall and both of them got a sinking feeling. Wren stopped. "I don't think it went very well, do you?"

"We'll soon know. By tomorrow morning, there might only be half a dozen of us left. It sounds like the place has emptied out already. What time is it?"

"Wren looked at her watch. "It's just after nine," she replied.

"I've got a bad feeling about this."

"Me too," Wren said as they continued more slowly towards the exit. The doors were closed, which was something else unusual. During the daylight hours, they had nearly always been open. As Robyn took hold of the handle, they both inhaled deeply, readying themselves for whatever awaited them beyond.

She opened the door and both girls' eyes widened to see the squall of frantic activity. Georgie was sat on the steps just watching. Robyn and Wren sat down beside her, and the same bewildered smile broke across their faces, too.

"Erm…" Robyn said.

"Yeah," replied Georgie.

"So people didn't desert," Wren said.

"Quite the opposite."

The three of them watched as Stevenson, Dan, and two of the other guards each instructed their own groups of ten. The squads were made up of men and women alike, all doing their best to familiarise themselves with the weapons they held in their hands. On their unit leader's instructions, they occasionally brought the rifles up to their shoulders, sighted a target and pulled the trigger, releasing an imaginary bullet before bringing the rifle back down and awaiting further instructions.

The joiner had recruited a group of enthusiastic DIY amateurs, and together they were busy sawing and hammering outside the large garden shed that had become his workshop. Sheets of scrap metal were being bolted into place on the two gates by another group of workers.

"So, they're ready for a fight," Wren said.

"They will be soon," Georgie replied. "The woodwork brigade over there are making all sorts of things, but there's one guy whose job is to make spears and nothing else. You too are pretty impressive with your javelins; do you fancy giving people a couple of demos?"

"It's not like it's hard," Robyn said.

Wren leaned forward. "…Said the girl who killed a pair of perfectly good coveralls training in our back garden."

"That was different. That was for zombies."

"So is this. They need to know how to defend themselves. Whether it's a man or a monster, if they don't know what to do when the time comes, they're going to end up dead either way, aren't they?" Wren said.

Robyn let out a sigh. "Don't you ever get tired of being right?"

"I've got nothing to compare it to."

Georgie laughed. "So I can rely on both of you to put your teaching heads on tomorrow?"

"Does that mean we're not going out scavenging any longer?" Wren said.

Georgie went quiet and looked down at the ground.

"What does that mean?" Robyn asked.

"I want you two to stay here," she said.

"Why? What are you not telling us?"

"Look, we managed to convince people we could make this place like a fortress, with no small amount of help from our tradesmen. They told people how they could help fortify this place, how they could make it more easily defendable…"

"And?" Robyn asked.

"They gave a list of supplies they would need. It was either say we could get them and give people confidence, or say we couldn't and lose it," Georgie said.

"So…?" Robyn said.

"So we're heading to a huge DIY centre just outside of Perth."

Wren burst out laughing. "Yeah, good one. No, seriously…where are you going?"

Georgie just looked at her. "That's insane," Robyn said.

"We're taking one of the lorries and the seven and a half tonner. There's going to be myself and Stevenson, ten guards and another ten men who are going to help us load everything."

"You haven't thought this through," Wren said.

"Look, if we don't get supplies, people will think Stevenson and me are full of crap and then we will start getting people leaving here in droves." She nodded her head towards the joiner. "Ed's a bit more than just a joiner; he's a master carpenter. He carries the same respect as anybody in this village. People listened to him when he spoke; he won them over for us. It's up to me and Stevenson to come through now."

"I still say you've not thought this through. You'll be on the A9, a big open road that any bandits can see and hear you coming on for a long way in either direction. You'll be moving slow because you've got a lorry...which everybody will assume is full of swag. You're heading to the outskirts of a place with a population in excess of forty thousand people...oh...and did I mention we're in the middle of a zombie apocalypse? This is a really bad plan. You need to rethink," Wren said, standing up.

"Wren's right. It's crazy," added Robyn.

"I've been through all the options, over and over. We need to do this," Georgie said, almost apologetically. "If there was an easier way, a safer way, I'd take it."

"Right, okay...well, we're definitely coming with you then," Wren said.

"Eh?" Robyn replied.

"Look, I know you girls have—"

"This isn't up for debate. You think rifles will protect you out there? They're a last resort, not a first choice. They're what you need when you're making a run for it and there's no other hope. If you show up and there are a handful of those things, you need to take them out quickly and quietly. You start shooting the place up and everything in earshot will come down on you like a plague of locusts," Wren said.

Georgie looked at Wren for a moment then back to the groups who were practising with the rifles. "I don't understand," she said distantly.

"You don't understand what?" Wren asked.

"How the world can fall apart and instead of banding together, instead of fighting those monsters together, some people can still be just out for themselves."

"What? You thought the end of the world would mean a change in human nature? Have you ever read The Selfish Gene?" Wren asked.

"Oh god...now you've started something," Robyn said under her breath.

"My point is...nothing can change what's truly inside someone," Wren said.

"That's a cheery thought," Georgie said.

"It's the truth. And the thing is, if this place isn't prepared, if these people aren't ready, then you're going to find out just how true. Look, we're coming with you tomorrow. You can try and argue as much as you like, but it's the smart play."

A group of twelve people appeared from around the side of the house. They were carrying cases and holdalls. "We've got all the stuff moved out. It's under some tarpaulin at the back," one of them said to Georgie as they all ascended the steps.

Georgie stood up. "Thank you. I really appreciate it," she said.

"Happy to help," replied the man. Just bring it back safe," he said, smiling; then he led the rest of the group through the doors and into the Manor.

"What was all that about?" Robyn asked.

"They live in the lorry we're taking tomorrow. Nice family...they volunteered."

"So what time are we setting off?" Wren said.

Georgie looked at her. "I don't suppose I can talk you out of this, can I?" she asked.

"You know I'm talking sense."

"We move out from here at four-thirty."

"In the morning?" Robyn asked, horrified. "Four-thirty in the morning?"

Georgie couldn't help but laugh. "Yes."

"Ugh!" She shoved Wren hard. "I hate you," Robyn said, heading back into the Manor.

"I still don't like this, just so you know," Wren said. "I think it's a flawed plan."

"You don't like it, I don't like it, Stevenson doesn't like it, but it's what needs to be done."

"I'm going to go catch a few hours' sleep," Wren said.

"That's probably a good idea. It's going to be a long day for everybody tomorrow."

"Well...let's hope it is," she replied, heading back into the mansion.

When she reached her apartment, Robyn was sat on the couch with a big bag of crisps. "I've never met anyone who can eat so much junk food and hardly put on any weight."

"I'm comfort eating," Robyn replied, spitting small fragments of crisps over her t-shirt.

"Y'know, we've got fresh fruit, we've got some nice veg too. Fresh, organically grown carrots. They're really sweet."

"Good. You eat your carrots—I'm fine with these. Anyway, crisps are made from potatoes...potatoes are veg," she said, stuffing another handful into her mouth.

Wren disappeared into the kitchen and came back out with another bag of crisps. She flopped down into the armchair, opened the bag up and shovelled a handful into her mouth. "I thought you wanted a carrot," Robyn said.

"Yeah...I figured if this was going to be my last meal then...y'know."

"It's mental...you do know that, don't you? The whole plan. We've been out there, Wren. Can you imagine what it's going to be like?"

"Yeah, I can."

"So why did you volunteer us?"

"Because…"

"Because why?"

"I…I guess I feel responsible."

"For what?"

"For putting Georgie in this position." Wren replied.

"Look. Georgie's a grown woman. Stevenson's a grown man, they make their own decisions." Robyn shoved another handful of crisps into her mouth.

"I'm sorry I volunteered us."

Robyn smiled. "Like I didn't see it coming," she said, spitting more crisps down her front.

Wren laughed. "You really are a pig."

Robyn opened her jaws wide to reveal a mushed-up mound of soggy yellow crisps on her tongue. "What?"

Wren started giggling and lost some of the food from her own mouth in the process. "You are so gross," she said, to which Robyn stuck her tongue right out, still covered in the globby mixture.

She started laughing too, then the sodden crisps slid from her mouth, landing on her chest. She looked down at the sludgy concoction and pulled a horrified face. Wren creased over; tears running down her face. Robyn continued to look at her chest for a moment, then grabbed the gooey potato snack in one hand and shoved it back into her mouth, wiping her hand clean on her stomach. "No point in being wasteful," she said, but it sounded like: "nu pon bing wafle."

Wren dropped from her armchair onto the floor, hysterical; more crisps fell out of her own mouth as she watched her sister. When she calmed a little, she repeated, "You are so, so gross."

Robyn screwed her face up, lifted her lower body off the couch and broke wind, at which Wren began to howl with laughter again. Robyn joined in. They both laughed much longer than the joke deserved, but quietly, behind their thoughts, they knew this could be the last laugh they ever shared.

*

"This is alright isn't it?" Cadmore said, changing into one of the fresh t-shirts that had just been delivered.

"Oh yeah, this is just peachy," Strand replied, sitting down at the far end of the caravan, watching a group of roughnecks two doors up playing cards.

"I can't believe you're not coming out tonight. Rollins said he was going to take us to the Fun House," Cadmore said, smiling.

"I did get shot today y'know," Strand replied, gesturing towards his arm.

"Yeah...how is your arm?"

"Painful."

"Well maybe a bit of entertainment would take your mind off it. I was speaking to one of the other guys and he says—"

"You do realise, those women aren't there by choice, don't you?"

"Look, like this guy said, out there, they'd be dead in a minute. In here, they get a roof over their heads, they're safe, they don't have to worry about getting attacked by zombies or nothing, and they get fed. You saw what happened in Aberfeldy. They're lucky to be alive."

"You really think you can justify it like that?"

"Here…you're not turning gay on me, are you, cos I want another caravan if you are," Cadmore said laughing.

"Forget it. It's pointless talking to you."

Cadmore was about to respond when there were three knocks on the door. He opened it and Rollins was standing there with two other men. "You ready?" Rollins asked.

"Yeah, Strand's stopping here."

Rollins peeked his head around the corner. "What's up? We've come to show you the nightlife."

"My arm's hurting like a bitch. I'm going to take some more painkillers and get some shut-eye."

"Fair enough," Rollins replied. "We'll be by for you at seven tomorrow morning; be ready."

"I'll be waiting," Strand replied as Cadmore excitedly stepped out into the open. They closed the door behind them and Strand watched as they disappeared through the maze of caravans. Raised voices immediately dragged his attention back to the card game, and one of the men jumped to his feet. Another stood up more slowly and menacingly; for a second, it looked like a full-scale fight would break out, but then one of the other players stood and calmed the situation down. A moment later they were all laughing again.

Strand stood up and closed all the curtains, blocking the world out, hoping that when he opened his eyes the next morning, this would all have been some kind of horrible dream. But in his heart, he knew it was real. He was in Hell, and there was worse to come.

9

"Bobbi," Wren said, gently rousing her sister. "Bobbi...it's four o'clock." It was already light outside, but a thousand suns shining through the thin curtains would struggle to wake Robyn from her sleep. Wren shook her a little harder.

Robyn groaned but did not say anything. Wren shook her again, and this time one eye opened. "Whaaat?" she asked.

"It's time."

"Time for what?"

"Time for us to get up."

"What time is it?"

"Four o'clock."

"That's still the middle of the night."

"I know, Bobbi, but we've got to get ready."

"Just five more minutes," Robyn said, turning onto her side.

Wren's head dropped. "I know you're going to hate me for doing this, but—" she ripped the quilt off in one swift movement.

Robyn did not leap up and grab her, as she'd expected, she just stayed there for a moment in exactly the same position before rolling onto her back and then onto her side to face Wren, who was standing over the bed, ready to run. "Coffee...I need coffee."

"The kettle's just boiling."

"Okay," Robyn said, slowly swinging her legs over the side.

The girls had their coffee, got washed and dressed in virtual silence, and at four twenty-five, they put on their rucksacks, gathered their weapons, and headed out to the courtyard. The vehicle engines were already running. The sisters headed to the minibus and were about to climb in when Georgie called over to them. "Hey...girls!"

They both looked across to the truck that had gone out on previous scavenger missions. Georgie was in the driving seat, leaning out of the window, beckoning them.

"What are you doing, driving this?" Wren asked.

"I thought as you're our stealth team, it would make more sense for you to be in an elevated position where you can see everything that's going on," Georgie said.

"What's the real reason?" Robyn asked.

"I didn't fancy being stuck in a cramped minibus with a bunch of blokes farting and burping for an hour there and an hour back."

"Good call," Robyn replied.

The pair walked around to the passenger side. They removed their rucksacks and Robyn took her quivers off, too. They carefully placed them in the footwell before climbing up to take their seats. Georgie wound down the passenger window so Wren could feed the long javelin through. Two minutes later, the metal patchwork entrance gates swung open and Georgie led the three-strong convoy out. They turned right onto the road, and they were on their way.

Rabbits scurried across their path as they drove, and there was not one thing in sight to suggest that the world had come to an end, until they hit the outskirts of Aberfeldy. Suddenly, the brief illusion of normality that had gently eased them into the morning came crashing down around them as the by now familiar sight of a town that had gone to Hell surrounded them.

On the other side of Aberfeldy, despite the early hour, they immediately became more watchful. It was almost as if they were crossing an invisible line into enemy territory. The sight of what had happened at the farm had ingrained itself deeply into their minds, and so they looked for threats behind every wall, on every corner.

They all breathed a sigh of relief as the convoy moved onto the A9. The road was clear and now, rather than carefully negotiating country lanes, they were hurtling along at seventy miles per hour.

"Well, if it's as clear as this at the DIY place, I'm going to be pretty happy," Georgie said, checking the mirrors to make sure the other two vehicles were keeping up.

"Oh yeah, I'm sure it will be, what with our luck and all," Robyn replied.

"This is a little freaky, isn't it?" Georgie said.

"How do you mean?" Robyn replied.

"The odd burnt-out wreck at the side of the road, the odd abandoned car…it's almost like the road has been cleared."

"It will have been," Wren replied. "Those men, the ones from Loch Uig, they'll have travelled up and down here a thousand times. They need the road clear so they can get to the next place to raid…. You do realise, they might have already been where we're going?"

"I'm hoping DIY wasn't big on their list of priorities," Georgie replied.

They carried on the rest of the journey, lost in their own thoughts, and it seemed like no time before Georgie was manoeuvring right, across a roundabout, on the final stretch towards the retail park where the DIY centre stood. She slowed down to make sure the other two vehicles were close behind her.

"We should pull up to do a reccy before we head into the car park," Wren said.

"Yeah, I was going to. Do me a favour, pull the binoculars out of the glove compartment, will you?" Georgie said.

"I mean...this is pretty out on a limb," Robyn said. "No houses around here; it looks like it should be safe."

"Yeah," Wren said, "Looks like."

Georgie pulled the handbrake on and kept the engine running, but climbed down from the cab, as did Robyn and Wren. Stevenson and another man joined them from one of the other vehicles as they walked up to the wire fence that encircled the vast retail complex.

"Crap!" Robyn said, seeing that a drive-through McDonald's had burned to the ground.

"Don't be too disappointed," Stevenson said, "I'm guessing they ran out of Big Macs a long time ago."

"No, not that. If there was a fire, that means that there will have been smoke. If there was smoke, then that could have drawn those things to the area," Robyn replied.

"Ah, yeah…I didn't think about that."

"Yeah, well don't worry Stevo, that's why you brought the big guns along," Robyn said, smiling.

Georgie remained silent. She had the binoculars up to her eyes and slowly panned them from side to side, but then stopped suddenly. "Okay, I see one, two, three, four...they're moving together as a pack. They're at the far end, near the electrical store."

"Four's nothing," Robyn replied.

"Don't get cocky," Wren said.

"What do you think?" Georgie said, turning to look at Stevenson.

"Well...erm...maybe if we...."

"You should send in the minibus first," interrupted Wren.

"What? Why?" Georgie said.

"For a start, it's armoured, and you've got that big snowplough thing attached to the front of it. It could easily take the four of them out, but more importantly, it can get out of there quickly if there's trouble. You don't want all three vehicles going in there before we know it's safe. You've never seen what happens when these things surround something. For all we know, there could be another two hundred zombies waiting behind one of the buildings," Wren said.

Stevenson and Georgie looked at each other, then back to Wren. "Anything else?" Stevenson asked.

"Isn't that enough for the time being?" Wren replied.

Stevenson let out a small chuckle. "Yeah, I suppose it is." He turned towards Georgie again. "Erm...what she said."

"Okay then," Georgie replied, "good luck."

They all took one final look towards the huge car park then walked back down the embankment to their waiting vehicles. Georgie stayed put while the armour-plated minibus swerved around her and turned left. She waited a few seconds and then she, too, pulled out, immediately checking her mirror to make sure the lorry was behind her. By the time her truck reached the entrance to the car park, Stevenson had already put his foot down and the minibus was hurtling over the tarmac with its engine roaring.

The three of them climbed down from the cab, and Wren brought the binoculars back up to her eyes. She saw the four creatures sprinting over the tarmac towards the speeding bus. Two seconds and it was all over. The flailing bodies of all four were flying through the air. One of the beasts rolled under the tyres, making the reinforced vehicle judder before it looped around in a wide circle and came to a halt. It waited there to see if any of the creatures rose. Three were perfectly still; their mangled bodies and skulls so badly damaged that even if they were not completely dead, any basic function was impossible.

The fourth lifted its head and began to drag itself towards the minibus. It scraped across the car park, a few inches at a time. Despite its broken bones, mashed-in face, and collapsed rib cage, it had lost none of its malevolent intent. The minibus engine revved loudly before its wheels screeched, causing grey-blue smoke to billow from the tyres. A second later, it was racing towards the clawing figure once more.

"Well, that seemed pretty easy," Georgie said.

"Do you hear that?" Wren asked

The head of the creature exploded against the front grille before its body flew back. It did not try to scramble to its feet again. "That's just the tyres. You tend to get more noise on hot days, the surface can sometimes—"

"No, not that." Wren dropped to her knees and put her head to the ground.

"Wren...what are you doing?"

Robyn began to turn in a circle. She and Wren had been here before. "Talk to me sis," she said.

Wren brought her head back up. She looked at the radio in Georgie's hand then looked at Georgie. "Get them out! Get them out of there now," she cried as she jumped back to her feet.

Before the words had come out of her mouth, a vast horde of creatures had emerged from around the far side of one of the retail outlets.

"Oh god!" Georgie said, hitting the talk button as she and the two girls ran back to the waiting vehicle. "Stevenson, get out of there. Get out of there! Hundreds of them are coming around the side of Perth Furnishings Warehouse."

For a moment, nothing happened, but then the wheels spun on the minibus again and it began moving— with all the creatures following it. The minibus was nearly at the exit to the carpark when it stopped.

"Georgie! Listen to me. We're going to lead them away, make sure they're a good distance from here. Wait until they're out of sight then head in. Over."

"That's mental! What if you run into trouble? You could get trapped. Over."

"We need those supplies. Don't worry, I'll make sure I take them far enough away before I head back here. Now back up and stay out of sight. Over and out." No sooner had Stevenson said the words than they heard the sound of the lorry reversing with its loud beep, beep, beep rising into the air.

Georgie, Wren and Robyn urgently looked towards the creatures to see if they had heard, but if they had, they were not interested; they were all homing in on the minibus.

"Come on girls," Georgie said, and the three of them ran back to the 7.5-tonne truck. Georgie carefully backed it down the hill, and when they were out of sight of the entrance, she wound down the window and turned off the engine.

The three of them sat there in a morbid silence as the sound of the horde's growls rose into the air. The pounding feet seemed to drum forever louder until finally, they began to diminish. When it was all but gone, Georgie started the engine again and a few seconds later the lorry's engine rumbled to life as well.

"It's working," came Stevenson's voice over the radio. "They're all following us."

The worried look remained on Georgie's face. "Just be careful," she replied. She placed the handset in the door pocket and the truck slowly began to move forward.

Georgie pulled the truck back into the car park and she immediately saw half a dozen stragglers. They were spread out and moving slowly. Each one was disabled in some way; maybe they had been trampled by the horde, maybe they had been differently-abled in life, either way, they just looked sad as they stumbled towards the truck. Georgie began to rev the engine.

"Don't bother," Wren said. "No point in risking damage to the truck just for these. We'll head over to the DIY store, and by the time they get there, Robyn and I can take them out easily."

"Okay, how do you want to do this?" Georgie asked as the truck came to a standstill next to the giant shop's trolley port.

Wren and Robyn just looked at each other, then Wren walked towards the creatures, making a point of looking back to the cab of the lorry and the men who were almost cowering behind the dashboard.

Whoosh, whoosh, whoosh, thud, crack, splat. In the blink of an eye, the first three creatures lay motionless on the floor. Wren approached the others, spinning the javelin like a baton twirler.

"Now she's just showing off," Robyn said with her bow raised and an arrow nocked ready.

"I think she's trying to prove a point," Georgie said, looking towards the frightened men in the truck.

"What point's that?"

"That she's got a bigger set of balls than that lot," Georgie replied, nodding towards the lorry.

"She didn't need to do anything to prove that."

"True enough," Georgie replied. She watched as Wren finished off the other three creatures then turned towards the entrance of the DIY store. Georgie signalled the all-clear, and the men climbed down from the cab. Two of them joined her, while a third walked to the back doors and opened them up, letting out the eight men who were going to do a lot of the heavy lifting.

One of the men from the cab pulled out a blow torch and cut straight through the lock securing the two metal-framed glass entrance doors together. He did the same with the inner doors, but did not open them.

"Let's get to work then," Georgie said, taking hold of the handle. She was about to tug the first door open when Robyn grabbed her arm.

"What are you doing?"

"What do you think I'm doing?" Georgie replied.

"We don't go into any building without making sure it's clear," she said.

"But it was locked," Georgie replied.

"Doesn't matter," Wren said, rejoining them.

The men who had been ready to enter the huge warehouse were now a little edgy once more. They looked around at each other nervously. All they had been told was that they would be needed for their muscle, to load the lorry. There had been nothing about coming into contact with these creatures.

"Ready?" Robyn asked, looking at Wren.

"Ready," Wren replied.

Robyn swung the inner door open and Wren immediately began to hammer her javelin against the metal frame. "Hey! Hey! Is there anybody here? Hey! Hey!"

Both girls waited, but nothing came to greet them. "Okay," Wren said as they both started to head inside.

"Girls, what are you doing?" Georgie asked.

"Just cos nothing came at us, it doesn't mean there's nothing in here. We need to check it," Robyn said.

"Alright, but I'm coming with you," she said, raising her rifle.

"Hold on a minute," Ron, the lorry driver who had been on the ill-fated mission to the mill, said. "None of us have got any weapons. We were just meant to be driving and loading. What if more of those things come back?"

Georgie handed him the rifle. "The narrow end is the one that the bullet comes out of," she said before turning her back on the men and heading into the warehouse after Robyn and Wren. She removed her sidearm and raised it. "Where do you want to start?"

"How about aisle one?" Wren said.

"Dumb question, I suppose," Georgie replied.

The three of them slowly headed down to the far end of the warehouse. Robyn had her bow raised and ready, while Wren walked with her javelin by her side, occasionally tapping the ground with it as she went along. "Sorry in advance if any of those blokes are friends of yours, but what a bunch of wusses!" Robyn said.

"No friends of mine," Georgie said as they reached the end of the walkway and paused before springing around the corner. Relief swept over them as they saw the long, wide aisle was clear. They began to walk up it slowly, their heads occasionally flicking to the left to make sure the other cross aisles were clear.

"I think we're going to be okay. The noise we made at the door was plenty to rouse any of them," Robyn said.

"You can never be too careful," Wren said, continuing to scour every corner.

"Well, you certainly can't," Georgie said.

Wren smiled. "The enlightened ruler is heedful, and the good general is full of caution."

"Oh god. Is there anything you don't have a quote for?" Robyn said.

"Was that Sun Tzu you just quoted?" Georgie said as they continued along the aisle.

"Yeah, my coach made me read The Art of War until I had most of it memorised."

"Smart man," Georgie replied.

"Yeah...he might have been an old perv, but he was a pretty good coach."

"Oh, come on sis, we're wasting time, this place is obviously empt—"

Suddenly, one of the walls shook as a huge crash sounded from the loading bay.

10

"So how many teams like this one are there?" Strand asked Rollins as the pair of them carried another crate of tins out of the service station.

"We've got a few smaller ones. TJ tends to lead out the bigger expeditions, but he's waiting for his arm to heal up before he heads out again. Another few days and he should be okay."

"Bigger expeditions?"

"Yeah. They went further south recently, came back with lorry loads of all sorts. When they go out they sap an area dry...course, they've got the resources to do it. It's not like we could empty a town with what we've got is it?" Rollins asked.

"Suppose not, no."

"Anyway, your arm seems a lot better," Rollins said, pointing to the bandages.

"Yeah, the painkillers help, and it seems to be working okay."

"So, an early night did you good?" Rollins said, with a lingering stare.

"World of good."

"Your pal's settling in well. Made a couple of mates last night." He looked towards Cadmore, who was laughing with one of the other men.

"Yeah, he's in his element."

"And what about you? Are you in your element?"

A thin smile appeared on Strand's lips. "Look, Cadmore and I are very different. He's easily impressed. You put him in a room with colourful lights and loud music and he'll be happy, apocalypse or no. I just like taking things a little slower."

"Fair enough," replied Rollins, as they lifted the crate into the back of the wagon.

*

Stevenson kept checking the mirror as the rest of the men in the minibus became increasingly nervous. "I hope you know where you're going," said one of them. "If you take us down the wrong street we could be royally stuffed."

"Yeah, thanks for that, Dawkins, like I need reminding."

"Just saying."

"Yeah, well, the next time you just wanna say something, jot it down and when we get back home."

"How far have we come?" asked another of the men.

"Just over a mile," Stevenson replied.

"Isn't that far enough?"

"I'm not taking any risks. I want to make sure there is plenty of distance between them and that DIY store by the time we get back there. The last thing we need is to be caught unawares."

The minibus fell silent again and Stevenson was sure he could almost hear the men's skin prickle as they looked through the letterbox gaps in the armour to watch the army of creatures pursuing them.

*

"What the hell was that?" Georgie said, her other hand closing around the Glock 17 as well.

"Told you," Wren said, glancing towards Robyn before training her eyes towards the wide, plastic swing doors that led into the storage depot and loading bay.

"One day...one day you're going to be wrong and I will be all over you like a rash," Robyn said, as the three women faced the warehouse entrance. She took a breath, pulled back the bowstring to firing position, and brought the sight window up to her eye.

"You ready?" Wren asked, looking towards Georgie, then Robyn.

"Ready!" Robyn replied.

Wren pushed the doors open and they walked through, slowly at first. There was plenty of illumination, thanks to the giant skylights that punctuated the corrugated steel roof. "Get ready to run if there's a load of them," she whispered. "Aaarrrggghhh!". Her cry echoed around the depot and all three women tensed, ready for the attack. When nothing came, they looked towards one another and immediately relaxed a little.

"Hey! Hey! Free meat, come and get it!" shouted Robyn.

"Bet that takes you back to every party you've been to, doesn't it?" Wren said.

They started to move forward slowly, carefully checking every inch, looking for anything out of place. Just then, they saw a set of safety steps lying on its side in between two giant rows of racking. All three of them looked up, and that's when they saw two small heads appear.

"Hi!" Georgie said, immediately lowering the javelin. "What are you doing up there?"

The boy looked at his sister and then back down at the stranger. "Dad said if we heard anything, we had to climb onto the rack and push the steps away."

"Okay, and where's your dad?"

"Him and Mum went out yesterday. Aunty Jean and Uncle Paul were coming, but they never showed up. Mum wanted to go find them. They're not back yet."

Georgie, Wren and Robyn all looked at one another. "But what are you doing in here?" Georgie gestured around the warehouse.

"Dad's the manager here. He said it was safer than where we lived, and that's why Aunty Jean was coming too."

"Let's get you down from there, shall we? You don't have to worry about us; we're not going to hurt you."

Wren and Robyn hoisted the big set of wheeled safety steps upright, and Wren climbed up to help the two children from the shelf. When they were safely down on the ground, the little girl burst into tears. "I want my mummy!"

"It's alright; she'll be back soon," said the boy.

"How old are you?" Georgie asked.

"I'm nine…my sister's five. Dad said that I was in charge of the place until he got back, but him and mum have been gone a long time."

"Tell you what, why don't you come outside with us and you can meet the rest of our friends. Don't worry; we'll look after you until your mum and dad get back."

The little boy took his sister's hand and then grabbed hold of Georgie's. "Okay," he said.

*

Stevenson looked at the reading on the mileometer and slowly nodded to himself. Up ahead there was a sign for a large industrial estate. He checked his mirrors and slowed a little more.

"What the hell are you doing? They're nearly on us as it is," cried one of the men.

"Keep your skirt on, Moretti. I want to make sure we don't lose any of them; we're about to start heading back."

"About bloody time," Moretti replied.

Stevenson brought the radio up to his mouth and hit the talk button. "Georgie, we're about two miles out. I'm going to ditch these ugly mugs and head back to you. Everything okay there? Over."

"Erm…more or less...you'll see when you get back. Over."

"You're worrying me. What's wrong? Over"

"No...nothing's wrong...it's just easier for you to see than for me to explain. See you soon. Over and out."

Stevenson looked down at the handset, shrugged, and then placed it back in the side compartment. He took the left turn onto the industrial estate as slowly as he could to make sure the minibus stayed in sight for as long as possible. Nervous mutters began to circulate between the men, who were crowding around the small slits in the back doors so they could witness the carnival of horrors that was pursuing them.

The minibus carried on for another fifty metres, and the creatures appeared to be gaining all the time.

"Jesus, Stevo, if you slow down anymore they're going to be in here with us."

"You're like an old woman, Moretti," he said, smiling before applying more pressure to the accelerator. The engine began to sing a sweeter song as the gap between the horde and the minibus grew. Relieved sighs and breaths became audible in the back of the bus as they watched the creatures grow smaller with each second that passed.

Stevenson slowed again to turn right, but his growing smile vanished as another multitude of beasts were already halfway down this road—heading straight towards them. He jammed on the brakes, and above their screech, Moretti's high-pitched chant of, "Oh shit! Oh shit! Oh shit!" was all he could hear. He slammed the gear stick into reverse, making a cringe-worthy grating sound.

"Don't stall, don't stall, don't stall," he hissed through clenched teeth as he rejoined the other street. He moved into first gear, his foot so far down on the clutch he thought it might break through the floorboard. Then he pushed his right foot down on the accelerator, bringing his left up slowly. There was a loud whirring sound and his heart stuttered, but as the minibus reluctantly began to gain speed, he dared look in the mirror. The creatures were still in hot pursuit, and now dozens more joined them as they stormed out of the side street.

"Faster. Faster, Stevo!" a voice shouted.

Stevenson put his foot down hard, moving up through third and into fourth gear. He looked again in the mirrors; they were breaking free, but right now they were heading further into the industrial estate, and they needed to head the other way. "What did that sign say?" he shouted, seeing just the back of it in his mirror. "What did that sign say?" he asked again.

There were mutters, but finally Moretti was the one who shouted back, "None of us saw it."

"Bloody brilliant," he spat. "Right, lads—hold on to your nads!". The tyres squealed once more as Stevenson applied the brakes and the minibus took the tight right turn. For a second it felt like he had misjudged and the whole bus was going to tip, but then the danger was over as all four tyres were gripping the road firmly. He continued to accelerate, and a small cheer went up behind him.

Two more creatures ran out from between buildings. They flung themselves at the vehicle, and their bodies bounced off the bonnet like they were made of rubber. They flew through the air, and Stevenson watched them crash against the tarmac in his wing-mirror as the army of creatures began to appear from around the corner. They had lost none of their speed or menace as they hurtled down the road after the minibus.

There was a T-junction ahead; turning left would take them further into the estate, right would point them back in the direction of the main road.

"There's more of 'em," shouted a voice as a mob of monstrous figures emerged from behind buildings and out of car parks.

"Okay lads…this is a tight one again," Stevenson said, braking and turning the wheel right. This time, the manoeuvre was more controlled; there were no screeching tyres, and he was able to accelerate faster. It took his brain a moment to catch up to his eyes to understand that all that lay ahead was a dead-end. "Shit! Shit! Shit!" he screamed, mounting the curb on the left-hand side of the road in order to do a U-Turn before the horde emerged. He pulled the wheel over hard.

"We're going to tip," shouted one of the men before a few others quickly shifted their body weight in an effort to counter the momentum. It worked; the minibus held, albeit precariously.

Stevenson let out a breath. He kept the wheel in a right lock, taking his foot off the gas just a little. They were almost round, almost pointing towards freedom, when the front left wheel glanced against the curb.

Suddenly, a second seemed to last a minute. They could all feel the minibus leaning beyond the point of no return. The Devil himself could not have choreographed a more terrifying moment. As the engine whirred hopelessly, the minibus continued to tip, and that's when the creatures began to appear from around the corner like a malevolent shroud of torment and horror.

The vehicle finally crashed onto its side; multiple yelps of pain filled the bus as bodies smashed against seats, metal, and other bodies. Within a few seconds, a dark curtain of movement had encircled the minibus. The sturdy metal plating over the windows and the doors were secure enough, but all these things needed was one point of entry and it was all over.

Faces began to press up against the metal grille that had been welded over the windscreen. Skin began to grate and mash causing bloody smears to appear over the glass. Frightened cries sounded as some of the men realised these terrifying images would be the last thing they would see.

A strong smell of urine filled the bus as one of the men lost control of his bladder, but there was no chastisement, there was no mockery. This was true terror, and the others knew it may not be long before they did the same.

Stevenson remained there, almost hanging by his seatbelt. He was frozen in horror too, as he watched the monstrous creatures vie for position, desperate to see, desperate to get to their trapped prize. The minibus rocked and as more and more beasts joined the horde; the metal of the bus shredded against the tarmac and concrete. Finally coming to his senses, he grabbed the radio. "Georgie, it's Stevenson...Over."

"Stevenson, this is Georgie, go ahead. Over."

"Georgie. We're screwed. The bus has gone over. We must have at least a couple hundred of those things around us. We're not going to last much longer. The grille's already starting to buckle. Get the stuff you need and get out fast. Over."

"What the hell are you talking about? Where are you?"

"Never mind that, listen to me—it's too late for us. You need to—"

Moretti snatched the radio. "Help us! You've got to help us. We're on the Springfield Trading Estate, about two miles towards Perth. You've got to help us."

Stevenson snatched the radio back. "Keep your mouth shut Moretti," he snapped. "Just get back safe. Get what you need and get back safe. Take care, Georgie. Over and out."

11

Georgie just stood, looking at the handset, hardly able to believe what she'd heard. "Oh my god," she said in a whisper.

"I want my mummy," the little girl cried again.

Georgie turned towards Wren and Robyn. "I've got to try and help them," she said.

"Didn't you hear the broadcast? By the time you get there, Georgie, it will probably be too late," Robyn replied.

They headed through the internal doors to find the men from the lorry waiting nervously. "It's all-clear; you can start work," Georgie said to Ron.

"We're not starting anything until the guards are back here. If those things come when we're loading, they could be on top of all of us in no time," he replied.

"Look. There's been a hitch. I'm heading out to bring them back now," Georgie said, downplaying the situation, knowing whatever happened, they needed the supplies.

"No, no, no, no, no," said another man. "That's not what was agreed. We were told we'd have the guards watching our back." Suddenly, he noticed the small children. "And where the hell did they come from?"

"I want my mummy!" the little girl cried again.

Georgie turned towards Ron. "Ron, come on, we're here for a reason. The sooner we get loaded, the sooner we get back."

"Yeah, and what happens if those things appear? What do you expect us to do then? No, Georgie. Go get the guards. That's what they're here for...to guard. When you're back, we'll start work."

"Too right," the other man said, as still more nodded.

Anger welled in Georgie's eyes as she looked at their faces. She eventually turned towards Wren. "Will you look after these two for me?" she asked, gesturing towards the children.

"You seriously think we'd let you go out there by yourself?"

Georgie looked back towards the men. "You've got children, haven't you, Ron?"

"Yeah, why?"

"Cos you've got two more until I'm back," she said, pushing the little girl towards him. "See you soon."

She was deaf to the protestations as she walked back out of the DIY centre. "How do they sleep at night?" Wren asked.

"I'd guess very well," Georgie replied. "Spineless wimps don't actually see themselves the way others see them. Things are always somebody else's problem. They are always the victims. The world's full of them."

"Not 'full of them,' not anymore," Robyn said as they climbed back into the truck. "Thankfully."

Georgie looked in the mirror to see Ron and the rest of the men just gawping towards them in disbelief. The little girl was still crying her eyes out, and the boy was looking around, desperately trying to find a friendly face. "I feel guilty leaving those kids with them."

"Better they're left here than where we're going," Wren replied.

"I suppose."

"So what's the plan?" Wren repeated.

"I'm flattered that you think I've got a plan, Wren. I heard what you heard on the radio. It'll probably be too late by the time we get there, but I can't just let those men die without trying anything," she said, starting the engine. The truck began to roll away and the bewildered faces of their loading team soon disappeared as Georgie drove out of the carpark and joined the main carriageway.

"If they're surrounded, it's going to be tough to get those things away from the minibus. When they smell blood, when they've got someone trapped, they pretty much ignore everything else," Wren said.

"So what are you telling me?" Georgie asked.

"Nothing, I'm just saying."

"I don't want problems, Wren, I want solutions." Wren looked a little hurt and sat back in the seat, hugging her javelin. No sooner had Georgie spoke than she regretted her words. She reached across and gave Wren's arm a squeeze. "I'm sorry. I'm just..."

"It's alright. I understand," Wren said.

The truck sped down the road until Robyn shouted, "There...that sign...it says Springfield Industrial Estate."

Georgie squinted at a tall road-sign in the distance. "Wow, you've got some eyes, kiddo," she said, beginning to apply the brake. She turned left onto the estate and pulled up next to the curb.

*

The minibus continued to shift along the ground as the creatures shoved and jostled, desperate to gain access to the shouting, screaming, crying prey within.

Stevenson had climbed into the back with the other men. Despite the bus being on its side and chaos filling the very air around them, they pointed their rifles towards the front. The grille covering the windscreen had begun to bend and buckle even more, and each time there was a surge forward, and the minibus scraped a bit further along the tarmac, the men applied a little more pressure to their triggers.

Then it came, the sound they had dreaded. The sound that heralded the beginning of the end. If they closed their eyes, they could be forgiven for thinking it was a thick piece of velvet being ripped apart, but alas, their eyes were wide open. They all watched as the crack spread across the windscreen from corner to corner. The heavy wire grille had held for as long as it could, but now the weight and force of these relentless beasts had begun to shatter its integrity.

"Okay," Stevenson began, "remember, headshots only, guys," he said as another split began to run through the glass. He could hear one of the men behind him sobbing. He couldn't blame him; he felt like crying himself. Who wouldn't?

The radio suddenly hissed. "Stevenson, this is Georgie. Over." He looked at it in the relative darkness, its little red light like a huge, shining beacon.

"Georgie—this is Stevenson, go ahead. Over"

"We're here. We've just pulled into the estate. Where are you? Over."

"I told you not to come," he replied, releasing the talk button once again.

"Yeah, well, sue me. Where are you?"

"They're almost inside, Georgie."

"Where the hell are you!?" she shouted.

Moretti dragged the radio from Stevenson's hand again. "Georgie...Georgie, second right and right again at the end of the street. Hurry...please...hurry."

Stevenson grabbed the radio back from Moretti and hit the talk button. "Georgie? Georgie?" but there was no response.

*

Georgie put her foot down on the accelerator, concentrating on the road ahead while Robyn and Wren scoured their surrounds, looking for signs of the undead. The truck took the second right, and very soon, the T-junction came into view. She skidded to a stop at the end of the road, the engine only barely audible over the excited growls of the huge throng of creatures surrounding the toppled bus.

"Here goes nothing," she said, smashing the heel of her palm against the horn.

A few creatures glanced in her direction, but for now, the sights, sounds, and excitement of the rest of the horde was far too much of a draw for them to go chasing off down the street. Georgie pressed hard on the horn again and even fewer creatures looked up this time.

"Turn left," Wren said.

"What?" replied Georgie.

"Turn left—now."

"I don't understand; why aren't they coming after us?"

"Because they've got them all within reach. They can probably smell them like animals smelling their prey. Now turn left, Georgie!"

There was pain, sadness, and confusion on Georgie's face. She did not have an answer. She thought the creatures would have simply chased after them, giving the trapped men enough time to escape. She steered the truck left and started travelling up the street, away from the minibus. Her expression grew sadder as the shoving, heaving mass of bodies grew smaller in the wing mirror. "I thought they'd follow us," she said almost under her breath.

"Concentrate, Georgie," Wren said, looking at the mileometer reading on the dashboard. Georgie dragged her eyes back to the road ahead, not really understanding why she was following orders from a fifteen-year-old girl, not understanding why the zombies weren't following her, not understanding anything at that moment in time, but just doing. Doing…something…instead of nothing.

"What are we doing?" Robyn demanded.

"Okay, turn left here," Wren said, ignoring her sister's question.

Georgie took one last look in the mirror and lost sight of the minibus as the truck turned. Tears began to roll down her face. Everything had gone to plan in her head, and as more tears came, she eased her foot off the gas pedal.

"Wren, tell me—"

"Faster Georgie! Concentrate!"

Georgie looked across towards Wren and the vehicle began to move marginally quicker. Wren kept her eyes glued to the dashboard gauges.

"Wren! Tell me what's going on," Robyn said angrily.

"In a minute," she said. "At the end of the road, turn left."

Georgie let out a long shuddering sigh as her tears continued. "Okay," she said, weakly. They were heading back out of the trading estate.

Those poor men. All dead because of my hair-brained scheme.

The main road they had turned in from was in sight. She would soon be heading back to the DIY superstore. *The Manor will not get its supplies, I will be going back, minus Stevenson and without the guards, minus several guns, and people will begin to lose heart. By tomorrow morning, there will be a mass exodus. Everybody will be ruing the day that I—*

"Left...turn left now!" Wren demanded.

Georgie suddenly roused from her thoughts as she pulled back onto the road they had been on a couple of minutes earlier. "What...what are we doing?" she asked as they carried on towards the T-junction.

"Listen to me, both of you. Those things aren't going to leave that bus unless we give them a better proposition," Wren said.

"A better proposition? What are you on about?" Robyn asked, irritated.

"Those things aren't going to come chasing after a vehicle when they've got men trapped just at the end of their fingertips. But if they've got live bait shouting and screaming at them, they will."

"No way are you going out there," Robyn said.

"That's mad, Wren. I'm not going to risk losing you as well," Georgie said, wiping the tears from her face.

"Look. I measured out how far it was. It's just over half a mile. When I was competing I could do the eight hundred in two minutes twelve. That means you've got about two and a half minutes for me to lead them off, get those guys out, then meet me back on the main road through the trading estate."

"Oh, yeah. And what if you trip? What if more of those things are lurking somewhere? I'm down one sister. No way. Just get that stupid idea out of your head."

"Look. We don't have time to argue. I love you," she said, grabbing Robyn and kissing her. She reached across and took Georgie's gun from the well in between the seats, opened the door, and jumped down.

"Nooo!" Robyn cried as Wren ran out into the middle of the street. She gestured for Georgie to back up out of sight, and Georgie, with no time now to argue, began to reverse the truck up, still in shock.

Wren watched until it was sufficiently far enough away not to be a potential distraction to any of the beasts, then she looked towards the mass of moving bodies surrounding the minibus.

"Hey! Hey! Over here!" she shouted at the top of her voice. Some of the creatures looked towards her, then Wren aimed the gun into the air and fired. The crack ricocheted up and down the street, and now all the creatures suddenly turned. As she had witnessed before, they began to move as one. Like a single flock of birds, they flew towards her, their prey in the minibus now forgotten as a living, breathing target stood out in the wide open.

Wren could feel the ground shake beneath her as the

creatures ran. She fired the gun again, then simply threw it onto the pavement. If a time came that she needed it from this point on, then it was already too late. There she stood in the middle of the road, the beasts not fifty metres from her and gaining with every stride. For all the bravado, for all the good intentions, she suddenly felt like a frightened little girl as she realised she was completely by herself. Sure that there were no stragglers, she turned and began to run faster than she had ever run before. She glanced to her left, but already something was amiss. There was no sign of the rescue vehicle.

12

The growls and pounding feet filled the air around Wren. She could not hear her own breathing, nor the sound of her own feet; all she could think about was running faster. All she could hope was that there was a good reason why the truck wasn't where it should have been and that everything would be back on track by the time she was due to meet them. For all Wren's strength and fitness, in the last weeks, she had not done any of the intensive training she was used to, and now, as she approached the end of the first strait, her thighs were already feeling the strain, and her breathing wasn't as it should be.

Wren turned the corner and threw another look down the street. By now, the truck should have moved into position, they should be getting the guards out then getting back to the main road through the estate to pick her up. There was no sign of anything—other than the hundreds of creatures chasing her. She kept her eyes in the direction of the minibus for as long as she could, but then it vanished from view, and with it, so did her hope.

*

"Georgie! What the hell is going on? Over," Stevenson asked, hitting the talk button on the radio.

There was no response.

"Where did they all go? Who fired that shot?" Moretti asked.

"How the hell should I know? But I'm not going to wait around for them to change their minds," Stevenson said, moving to the back of the minibus. He pulled the door lever and barged against it with his shoulder, spilling out onto the tarmac of the road, the other door folded out beneath him. He jumped to his feet, immediately bringing the rifle up to his shoulder, checking one side of the minibus, then the other to see if any of the monsters had decided to linger. He walked around the front as more of the guards emerged. "They're gone, all of them," he said, plucking the radio from his belt once more. "Georgie! Georgie! Where the hell are you?"

*

Wren continued to sprint with everything she had. She looked back to see the horde had gained ground. The lead creatures were just fifteen metres behind her now—one slip, one—then it happened. More interested in what was chasing her than where she was going, she hit a patch of oily tarmac. A second...two, she thrust her arms out, preparing to fall forward. She released a small whimper of fear, but then managed to straighten herself up and continue running. Her eyes fixed firmly on the road ahead, but that slip would have cost her even more of her narrow lead. The road ahead curved, and she knew that once she was around this bend, she would see the main thoroughfare. Seeing it and reaching it were two different things, though, as the pain in her thighs continued to intensify.

The creatures' feet were getting louder...she was slowing, despite all her efforts, she was slowing...and they weren't...not for a moment. Wren could feel the sweat dripping down her face, down her back. She could feel her lungs doing their best to suck in the air she needed, but what had seemed like such a good idea just a few moments before, now seemed like a death sentence.

How long have I been running? How long in minutes? Not long. How far left? Too far. She negotiated the bend, and there was the road. If she got to that, maybe Georgie and the truck would be waiting for her. But why wasn't the truck where it should have been earlier? Doubts, doubts, doubts…that's all that filled Wren's head now. On the road up ahead to her left, there was a parked car. Even from this distance, she could see the reflection; the creatures were mere feet away now. The leaders not much more than a couple of arm lengths. "Oh god!" she exhaled.

She focussed again, because focus was all she had. If she could just make it to the road ahead, at least that would be something, if she could just—

A figure in black suddenly appeared and walked into the middle of the street. For a split second, Wren thought it was the Grim Reaper carrying his scythe, getting ready to take her, but then she looked through the beads of sweat blurring her vision, and realised it was not the Angel of Death, but a different angel that stood there waiting for her. Bobbi!

Robyn placed an arrow against the nocking point of her bowstring and brought the sight window up to her eye. Wren was still a good distance away, and the chances of Robyn hitting a target so far back were not great, but the very fact that she was there gave Wren new purpose. Her sister had come to help her, come to share her burden. Wren carried on for a few seconds, then her eyes widened as Robyn released the first arrow.

The worst thing Wren could do now was change course. She kept on running and just hoped. The arrow whistled as it shot past her head. There was a thud and then more thuds as multiple creatures stumbled over the first one Robyn had brought down. She brought the bow up again and fired. Again, multiple creatures collapsed, and this time, Wren dared to shoot a glance back. Now there was a good gap, and still more creatures tripped and fell as others clumsily tried to climb to their feet.

Wren finally reached where Robyn was standing and they immediately pivoted left and began to run down the trading estate's main road. There was no sign of the truck, and Wren's heart began to beat even faster until the vehicle finally emerged from the side street up ahead and pulled onto the road. It rolled slowly forward as the back doors swung open and the rescued guards beckoned the two girls inside.

Wren and Robyn both threw glances back at the pursuing horde, but barring a serious mistake now, they were safe. They continued sprinting until they were right up to the back of the truck. Robyn handed her bow to one of the waiting hands before someone else grabbed a tight hold of her and pulled her up. Another hand reached out and took hold of Wren. The second they were on board, the doors closed and Moretti banged his palm against the wall of the truck three times, signalling the vehicle to speed up and get them out of there.

Wren looked towards Robyn with a huge grin on her face, but Robyn just glared at her sister. She took her bow back from the guard and walked to the front of the truck where she sat down in a corner. The men showered Wren with hugs and words of thanks, but all Wren could do was look towards her Robyn.

What had she done?

*

"I tell you what," said Rollins, "You finish off in here. I'll go and round the rest of the crew up and then we'll head up the road, yeah?"

"Yeah!" Strand said, placing the tins and packets of food from the amply stocked kitchen into the crate. The other siphoned the remaining diesel from the underground tank. They behaved like dim teenagers, and it was no surprise to Strand that Cadmore fitted right in. He placed the final packet in the crate and closed the lid.

The back door was open; it led out into a long-abandoned paddock, and then to the forest. No way could

Strand realistically throw in with this crowd. He was a lot of things, but he knew what they were, and he was most definitely not one of them. The stories Wren and Robyn had told about these men were true. They were bad...bad to the core. Nobody kept women in those conditions and justified it by saying at least they've got a roof over their heads. No, this was not for him. Strand was a selfish man, he knew that. He knew all his faults, but he had a sense of right and wrong. He'd hoped Cadmore had, too, but obviously he had been wrong.

He looked through the window and saw that the men had cracked open the refreshments. Rollins was leaning up against one of the diesel pumps with a bottle of water in his hand while another man was telling a story.

Strand opened the crate again. He had put a box of energy bars in there from a counter display which he now took out again and shoved into his pockets. He quickly looked around the kitchen. It was caked in filth. Anybody who had decided to eat at this roadside cafe had really taken their lives into their hands. He walked across to a knife rack and grabbed a handle. He pulled out a six-inch blade and tucked it in between the back of his jeans and his belt.

Strand went back to where he had been standing and looked out of the grimy window once more. The storyteller was still spinning his tale and Cadmore was sat there with that lopsided grin on his face. It was now or never. If he could just get a few minutes head start, there was no way they could catch— "Thought you'd decided to take a nap," Rollins said as he stood in the doorway regarding Strand.

Strand could feel his skin flushing red as if he had been caught in a lie. "No, just checking there's nothing we've missed."

Rollins folded his arms and in the light, his dark brown eyes almost looked black as he stared towards the other man. "Big energy barman, are you?" he said with a smirk on his face.

Strand looked down to his pockets, then looked back up with a sheepish grin on his face. "You caught me."

"Well, there's no harm skimming a couple of the spoils for ourselves. There've got to be some perks to the job, haven't there?"

"Yeah...I suppose there have."

Rollins unfolded his arms and walked across to where Strand stood. "Now how about you cut the bull and tell me exactly what's going on?"

"I don't know what you mean," Strand replied nervously.

"Let me put it like this. Your pal out there, he's with the programme. You...you're not. I think when we get back home, you, me and TJ are going to have a long chat," Rollins said with a menacing smile. He placed his hand on the butt of his sidearm as a gentle reminder that he had a gun and Strand didn't.

"Look, I've already told you, I just——"

"Yeah, you've already told me lots, but I think you're too clever by half. You've told me lots without telling me anything at all. I think it's time we all had a proper chat together...about this place you and Cadmore came from."

Strand could feel beads of sweat starting to trickle down his back. "Well, if Cadmore's with the programme, why not talk to him?"

"Oh I have...I have. He's told me an awful lot, but he's a bit of a lightweight. Poor attention to detail, and I know for a fact that's not your problem. You're not like him at all."

"No...you're right...I'm not." Strand pulled the knife from his belt and thrust it into Rollins' neck all the way up to the hilt. Rollins' eyes widened in horror as he gasped gurgling breaths. He tasted blood, he smelled blood and as he pulled his hands away from his throat, he saw blood, too...streams of it trickling over his fingers and running out of his hands. He looked down as far as the protruding blade would allow, to see a crimson fountain spurting onto the dirty tiled floor. He staggered a little and then collapsed. His eyes stared wide for a moment before closing forever.

Strand stood there in shock. He pulled the knife from his victim's neck and ran out the back door. He looked down at his blood-soaked hand, still not believing what he'd done.

Raucous laughter erupted from the men. Was that it? Was that the punchline to the joke? The end of their stories? Would they head inside to find Rollins there, bled out? Strand made it to the tree line and cast a look back. Nobody was following him yet, but he felt sure it wouldn't be long. He sprinted into the shade of the woods, zigging and zagging through the trees. Thirty more seconds and he looked back again; he could not see the service station at all now. If he couldn't see it, they couldn't see him. He continued to sprint flat out. I left the gun. I should have grabbed Rollins' gun. How many more mistakes would he make? For the time being, adrenalin was powering his strides and he had no intention of stopping until he was out of harm's way…but would he ever be out of harm's way again?

His only plan had been to run…no…that wasn't true. His plan had been to run and get back to the Manor. Whether they welcomed him or not, he had to warn them. He had to tell them what was coming.

13

The truck arrived back at the DIY depot and slowly the men began to emerge from the back of the lorry. They had been waiting...hiding, ready for a quick getaway at the first sign of trouble. As Georgie and Stevenson climbed out of the cab, they were immediately hit by a flurry of questions. The rest of the guards climbed down from the back of the truck, leaving just Robyn and Wren.

"Are you not going to talk to me, Bobbi?" Wren asked. The two girls had sat on opposite sides of the cargo compartment and Robyn had not cast a single glance in Wren's direction since the trading estate. Robyn looked up at Wren and just glared for a moment. "Come on, Bobbi...talk to me."

Robyn shook her head. "What the hell were you thinking?"

Wren's brow furrowed a little. "I wasn't...really...it was all I could come up with. There wasn't time to—"

"You could have been killed. You came so close."

"But I'm safe. I'm here, I'm okay."

"Not for a lack of trying, though. All those promises you made to me and they were just bull."

"What do you mean? What promises?"

"All that crap you said about 'it's just you and me, Bobbi. Nothing else matters, Bobbi,'" Robyn turned her head away.

"It doesn't."

"Well you could have fooled me, Wren. Do you have any idea how dangerous that was? How stupid? Course you don't, Miss Adrenalin Junkie. You just did it without a thought for me."

"I...those men...they…"

"Those men aren't us."

"Are you saying I should have left them to die?"

"I'm saying...I'm just saying...I can't lose you. That wasn't your decision to make. We're a team. I know I'm not as bright as you, but that doesn't mean that you get to make choices that affect both of us like that," Robyn began to cry.

Wren gently turned her sister's head around towards her, seeing the tears streaking her face. "I'm sorry. I'm sorry I didn't discuss it. My head just works differently. The communication side of it shuts down and everything focuses on the problem. I had a solution and that's all I could see. I'm sorry, Bobbi."

Robyn stood up, wiping the salty streams away with the heel of her palm. "Good. You should be."

Wren stood too. She stepped towards her sister and opened her arms for a hug. When Robyn did not reciprocate, she hugged her anyway. At first, Robyn's body was stiff, but eventually, she relaxed and put her arms around her little sister. "I'm sorry, Bobbi. I really am," Wren said.

"Okay. Just remember what I said," her voice still shivered.

"I will," she said, pulling away. "That was a hell of a shot, by the way," Wren added, smiling.

"What was?"

"That first one where you got the lead zombie."

"It was crap. I was aiming for you. I was at least a foot out."

Robyn picked up her bow and quivers and they both climbed out of the van. A heated discussion was going on between Ron and Stevenson.

"No," Stevenson said, "we're sticking to the plan."

"How can we stick to the plan if we're already one vehicle down? I say we should—"

"We're here already. The stuff we need is literally at our fingertips," Stevenson said, pointing into the DIY store.

The little girl was crying louder than ever now and the boy held her, looking on, wondering who had walked into their lives.

"None of that matters. The armoured minibus was our first line of defence. What if—"

"What if nothing. We haven't lost anyone. We've still got all our weapons," Stevenson spat back.

"I think we should put it to a vote. Who says we should head back to Cromore?" Ron asked, placing his hand into the air. A few more hands started going up behind him but stopped as Robyn spoke.

"You people are a disgrace," she said, marching forward angrily. "My sister risked her life to save the guards. My fifteen-year-old sister! While you stayed here cowering in the back of the lorry. Seriously, what kind of people are you? And now you're talking about going home empty-handed because the game's changed a little? Cos we've lost a vehicle? We were out there by ourselves...no vehicle, just the rucksacks on our backs. And you lot are bleating on like a bunch of scared children. None of you would last a day out there."

"Maybe not, but we won't—"

"I haven't finished," she said, interrupting Ron. "If we don't get those supplies, we're not going to be safe from attack, whether it's the living or the dead that come for us. If the Manor falls, you've got two choices. You stay there and die or you flee and try to live outside those walls." She looked around at the assembled men, then looked towards Georgie and Stevenson, whose mouths were gaping open.

"Let me tell you, I don't give any of you more than a couple of hours by yourselves on the streets. So make your decision. Have we come all this way for nothing? Did my sister risk her life for nothing? Are we going back to the Manor empty-handed? Or are we going to get what we came for and stop moaning like a bunch of spoilt brats?"

Ron's mouth dropped open too, as the rest of the men started to head into the store. "You've no right to speak to me or anyone like that."

"I've got every right," she said, taking a step towards him. Her glaring eyes and aggressive stance made him step back a little, despite being a good eight inches taller than her. "This is a new world now. If you don't like it, there's plenty of rope back at the Manor to hang yourself with. How dare you? How dare you, after what my sister did?" Something approaching a snarl appeared on Robyn's face. She took one final breath and then walked off, leaving Ron wondering what the hell had just happened, and who the hell they were really dealing with.

Wren had watched the whole thing from a few metres back and she was just as shocked as everyone else. She ran to catch up with her sister, who continued her march into the store.

"Erm...are you okay?" Wren asked.

"Yes I'm okay," Robyn snapped back.

"I was only asking."

Some of the bluster immediately left Robyn as the pair of them headed to a quiet corner. The other men had already split up, each gathering the supplies from the list that were designated to them. "I'm sorry, I shouldn't have snapped. It's just...these people. This is what I was saying, Wren. You risked your life for people like this."

"No I didn't. Stevenson's not like this. Georgie's not like this, and Dan's not. They're like us; they're good people, and there aren't too many left."

Robyn let out a long sigh. "I suppose I'm just a lot more selfish than you."

"Well I've always told you that," Wren replied, and suddenly they both laughed.

"Cow!"

"Bitch!" They laughed again. "But you were right, Bobbi. I shouldn't have just done it. I should have talked to you. I promise I won't do anything like that again."

"Okay. Let's head back out there and patrol. We don't want these guys complaining there's nobody to protect them," she said, smiling.

They both headed back outside. "That was some performance," Georgie said as they reached her.

"Had to be said," Robyn replied, shrugging.

"I've never seen a bunch of grown men put into their place like that before."

"My sister has never been one for subtlety," Wren replied.

"No, I can see that," Georgie replied, smiling.

"Are we taking them back with us?" Robyn nodded towards the two children.

"We can't exactly leave them here, can we?" Georgie replied.

"What if their parents do show up?"

"I don't think it's very likely, do you?"

"No, but it's possible," Robyn said.

"I'll leave them a sign, a note or something."

A smirk appeared on Robyn's face. "Saying what?"

"That their kids are safe and where they are."

"Yeah, good one," Robyn said, letting out a small laugh. "Seriously, what will you do?"

"I was being serious," Georgie replied.

"Jesus," Robyn said, shaking her head and marching off.

"I don't understand," Georgie said softly, looking towards Wren.

Wren watched her sister walk away before turning towards Georgie with a similarly confused look. "I'm sorry. I don't know what's wrong with her today."

"What did she mean?"

"Georgie, we can't be leaving signs or notes about where we are. What's to say that crowd from Loch Uig or some other gang won't get hold of it and turn up on our doorstep?"

"What an idiot. I wasn't thinking," she said, looking over towards the children once again. "So...we've got to whisk them off without the hope of them ever seeing their parents again?"

Wren placed a gentle hand on Georgie's arm. "Their parents are gone. The only option is taking them back with us. At least they can have some kind of life. These are hard times, and hard times call for tough decisions. You leave those to someone like Ron or the others, and they'll always take the easy way...the way that causes them the least problems. It's good that it's you making the choices. You'll agonise over all the hard stuff."

"So what you're saying is, you want to see me in perpetual agony?"

"Exactly," Wren said and they both laughed a little.

*

Strand had been running for what seemed like an age, but was probably closer to ten minutes. He doubled over, resting his hands on his knees as he tried to catch his breath. There had been no shouts or gunshots. He had cast frequent glances over his shoulder, but no posse had been hunting him. Knowing how lazy the men were, they would probably still be sat around the diesel pumps telling stories.

He had run into the woods, west, as best as he could tell, away from the road, away from the garage...Was that south-west? But then there was that stream, and he had to change direction for a little while. He kind of doubled back. "Oh crap!" he said, standing up straight and turning three hundred and sixty degrees. The forest looked the same in every direction. He needed to get back to the Manor to warn them, but which way was the Manor? Which way was the road, for that matter?

Strand looked up through the trees. The sun rose in the East, but that didn't really help him now as it sat high in the blue sky, laughing down at him. Suddenly, he heard an engine revving. It was a fair distance away, but he turned to the general direction of the sound and started walking. If he got to the road, at least he could figure things out from there. Maybe he could find a car and be back at the Manor by dinner time. For all the place's faults, for all the people's faults, he would rather be there than that hellhole Loch Uig.

He hoped he was walking in the right direction. The trees and bushes were becoming denser and some of these forests were huge. A sudden sound rose from a thicket, and Strand immediately began to run, not waiting to see what it was. He was in mid-stride as he looked back to watch a small flock of blackbirds rise into the shadowy forest. His nerves turned to laughter, but it was short-lived, as his foot caught in a tree root protruding from the ground. His body kept travelling, but his ankle stayed put, and Strand let out a howl of agony as his knee twisted and he crashed to the floor.

He contorted himself until he could grab hold of his foot with both hands and free it from the crooked manacle that had imprisoned him. He let out a stifled scream as the pain from his knee spasmed through him. Strand struggled to his feet and let out another grunt as he staggered across to a tree. This was it. He was done for. Whether living or dead, if anything came after him now, he was a goner.

14

In the end, it was just Robyn, Wren, and Stevenson who kept a vigil outside the DIY store while all the supplies were loaded up. Georgie had settled the two children in the staff canteen, occasionally heading back in to check on them. She had told them that she was going to leave a note for their parents in case they came back. Of course, it was a lie, and one that would weigh heavily on her, but it was the only option.

"Another ten minutes and we should be all done," Stevenson said with a smile. "I'll be glad to put this trip behind us."

"Tell me about it," Robyn replied.

"Listen girls, I just want to say—"

"You've already thanked us," Wren replied, cutting him off.

"Yeah well, thanks again," he said with a smile. "Look, I'm just going to check on Georgie. Yell if you need us."

"Will do," Wren said. "You've been quiet all day. What's wrong?" she asked, turning to her sister.

"I feel guilty, if you must know."

"Guilty? You?" Wren said. "The girl who once drew a monster on my backpack and scrawled 'Property of Nerdzilla' all over it? The girl who took a picture of me eating alone in Macdonald's and put it on her Facebook page with the title, My sister and all her mates enjoying a meal out? The girl who—"

"Okay, you don't need to remind me what a complete bitch I've been to you. I just feel guilty about being so selfish. About having a go at you when you were just trying to do the right thing."

"Don't. You're right—it's you and me. That's the most important thing."

Robyn looked back towards the lorry as a group of men threw some full bags of something that made a metallic clunk into the back, while two more climbed up to help position them. "Thanks, Wren."

"Listen. How about tomorrow we go foraging, just you and me. We'll head out early and have the day together."

"How early?" Robyn asked.

"Early."

"Is this what they mean when they say careful what you wish for?"

"Yep! It will just be you and me for the whole day. While everybody else is beavering away."

"Erm, don't you think people will be a bit peeved that we're heading out when there's so much to be done?"

"We're going scavenging for food. We're the only ones who know what to look for in the forests and can actually look after themselves. I'll explain it to Georgie and I'll make sure we're back in time to do our spear training classes in the evening," she said with a smirk on her face.

Robyn smiled. "I'd like that. It'll be like old times."

Wren took hold of Robyn's hand. "I'd like that too."

*

Strand had torn the sleeve from his shirt and bandaged it around his knee. He had managed to find a sturdy tree branch which he was able to use as a walking stick and now he continued his journey, hobbling through the forest like an old man. He hoped he was heading in the right direction. He heard something, and this time he knew it wasn't birds or any other woodland creatures. He heard twigs break, then he heard the familiar growl of one of the beasts...one of the undead.

Strand stopped dead in his tracks. Where was it? He slowly looked around, his foot thudding heavily against the soil as he turned. Then he caught movement. It was to his left. For the time being, the creatures...two of them, had not seen him. Should I stay still? Should I crouch? Try to get behind a tree and hide? Climb a tree? He had never had to face these things by himself before. The pain in his knee was forgotten for the moment as the two creatures continued past. He held his breath, terrified that his breathing would be heard. He swallowed hard and then fretted that even that would be enough to give away his position. One of the creatures paused and began to sniff the air.

This was it. They know I'm here. Strand backed up gradually; he would try and take cover behind a tree or some bushes, anything that would—his foot landed on a twig, the snap cracked through the silence like a whip.

"Oh god!"

*

Stevenson drove the truck while Georgie stayed in the back with the two children and the rest of the guards. Wren and Robyn kept their positions in the front; they were, after all, the Silent Snipers, as one of the guards had nicknamed them.

"I reckon we've got enough stuff in the back to build a new Manor, never mind enhance the existing one," Stevenson said as they pulled on to the A9. They had only travelled a short distance from the store, but there was already far less tension, far less anxiety in the air.

"Did we get everything on the list?" Wren asked.

"Yeah, and more besides. It was a good haul."

"I didn't see Georgie, is she okay?"

"Yeah. She was sort of down about lying to the little ones, but I told her she didn't have a choice. I'm sure there'll be lots of lousy calls to make over the next few months," Stevenson replied.

"Tell me about it," Robyn said, staring out of the window as the trees and fields began to whizz by.

"Hey, by the way, I spoke to Ed. He reckons he can build more bows. Do you think maybe you could show people how to use them...y'know, train them?"

"Sure, why not? He'd have to make some targets as well," Robyn replied.

"I'm sure he can manage that. He's a bit of a magician is Ed."

"Yeah," he reminds us of our Grandad. He could pretty much build anything he put his mind to as well."

"He's passed?" Stevenson asked looking across towards Robyn.

"He lived in Inverness; we were heading up there the day it all happened," Robyn said.

"Well, your genes came from somewhere. Who's to say he's not found a safe community of his own to settle down in?" Stevenson said.

"Yeah, who's to say?" Robyn replied sadly.

*

Even after hearing the sound of the twig snapping, Strand froze, hoping that somehow, the two creatures would not come after him. But within a heartbeat, they had both turned, and whereas before they seemed to be ambling through the woods, now they stormed towards him with purpose. The sound of the growls turned his blood to ice as he stood there with one bad knee, unable to run, barely able to walk. He pulled the knife from his belt and braced himself. If he was going to die, he wasn't going down without a fight.

Both creatures approached at the same time. He lifted the thick branch and despite the agonising pain that shot through his leg, he stayed upright. He grunted as he thrust the branch towards the chest of the creature to his right. The force of the collision nearly made him fall over, but he managed to keep his balance; instead, it was the beast that flew backwards.

Strand dropped the branch and swapped the knife to his other hand just as the second creature pounced. Strand's eyes widened as the monstrous figure dived towards him. It thrust its hands out, but Strand shunted his bodyweight onto his left foot, twisting as he went. He parried the beast's forearms, causing it to go crashing into a prickly bush.

The first creature was back on its feet and Strand turned again as he felt a twinge from the bolt wound in his arm. He kept a tight hold of his knife, despite the pain and let out a yelp as he applied pressure to his right foot once more. The beast lunged, and this time, Strand grabbed a fistful of cloth from its sweater in his left hand, while plunging the blade of the knife through its head.

For a brief moment, the pain he was feeling was forgotten and the euphoria of winning the battle with this monstrosity took over. Its eyelids closed as it collapsed to the floor, and he released the clutch he had on the beast's sweater.

He was about to turn around to face the other, when another agonising shot of pain ran through him. He felt the cold fingers of the creature sinking its nails deep into his neck and he let out a howl. Strand turned, and so much was the force of his attacker's strike, that it lost some of its balance and stumbled forward. Strand immediately put his left hand up to his neck and felt four welts. He brought his fingers back down and looked at them. Four lines of blood glistened on his hand.

"Aaarrrggghhh!" he screamed. The beast turned and lunged again, but this time, Strand was ready. He knocked the creature's arms away then thrust the blade through its eye socket. It fell like a tree, bouncing a little as it hit the ground. Tears began to run down his face as he looked at his left hand once more. It was all over now...it was all over.

*

Nearly everybody at the Manor gathered around as the vehicles came through the gate. There were concerned looks on all the faces. Three vehicles had gone out and only two had returned. Stevenson was the first to climb out and people immediately began to ask where the minibus was.

"It's okay!" he said, placing his hands up to placate them. "We ran into trouble, but no-one got hurt. We got all the supplies we needed and more."

This calmed the worried murmurs a little, but concerned looks continued to be exchanged at the news that there had been trouble. Stevenson opened the back of the truck and the guards climbed down first. Georgie passed to one of them first the little girl, then the boy, before jumping down herself. Pippa ran up to meet her and the pair flung their arms around each other. Georgie's parents walked up behind them.

The little girl, whose tears had finally subsided during the ride home began to cry again at the sight of all the new faces. Her brother clutched her hand in his, and Georgie broke the embrace with Pippa, realising there would be plenty of time for them later.

"Mum, Dad," she said, giving them brief hugs, "I'd like you to meet Robert and Amelia." Georgie pushed the boy and girl forward and a look of elation swept across Patricia's face to have more children to dote over. She crouched down and began talking to them. Almost immediately Amelia stopped crying again and Georgie smiled.

Robyn and Wren dismounted from the cab and were just about to head into the Manor when Ed, the carpenter, headed towards them with something wrapped in two small white sheets of cloth. "Erm, I made you girls something...just as a little thank you for everything you've done for us here."

Wren and Robyn looked at each other before each taking their gift.

"This is really kind of you Ed. There's no need though, it was—"

"Nonsense. It's just a small thing. An old man's way of saying thank you," he said with a warm smile.

Robyn unwrapped hers first. She gulped hard as she peeled back the final layer of cloth to find thirty beautifully crafted arrows. She picked one up and looked down the line. "They're beautiful," she said looking at the colourful plastic vanes. "Thank you."

Wren opened hers to find matching crossbow bolts. "These are lovely Ed, thank you so much."

He held his hands up, "No thanks needed, it's just my way of telling you, you're appreciated," he said, then turned to leave.

Wren and Robyn looked at their gifts long and hard, then carefully wrapped them once again. "Okay," Robyn said, "I have to admit, that was incredibly sweet. Maybe these people aren't as bad as I thought after all."

15

It was just after five a.m. when Robyn and Wren hoisted their rucksacks onto their shoulders.

They stepped out into the fresh morning air, and there was Georgie, sitting on the top step, waiting.

"You didn't think I'd let both of you go without saying goodbye, did you?" she asked without turning around.

"We're only having a day out," Wren said.

Georgie stood up and turned around. "Honestly?"

Robyn and Wren both looked puzzled. "Yes, honestly," Wren said.

Georgie looked at the rucksacks on their backs. They were not packed to the brim, in fact, they were nearly empty. "I thought…when you came to me yesterday and said you were going to be heading out early…I thought this is it. They're leaving us."

"What? Why?" Robyn asked.

"I saw how frustrated you were yesterday. Then when Robyn let rip…it felt like…like you didn't want to be here anymore."

"Honestly. If we ever decided to move on, we wouldn't go without saying goodbye. We're going foraging.

We're going to spend the day together, and then we're coming back," Wren said, smiling.

Georgie's face lit up. "I'm glad. You and Stevenson are the only real friends I've got here."

"I promise you, we're going to head into the woods, Wren is going to bore me stupid by telling me the Latin name for any weird plant or mushroom we come across. We'll grab a load of wild garlic and herbs and whatever else we can find, then we'll be back in time for dinner. This evening, we'll help you with the training, if you like," Robyn said.

"I'd like that," Georgie said.

"Good then," Wren replied.

The three of them hugged and the two sisters headed towards the gate. It clunked behind them and Robyn turned to Wren. "What was all that about? Talk about weird."

"Not so weird. You were pretty hacked off yesterday."

"So it's my fault?"

"You're the eldest. It's always your fault," Wren replied with a smirk. They carried on down the road. It was going to be a hot day. The birds were already chirping a morning chorus, and despite the hour, a relaxed smile eased its way onto Robyn's face.

They turned right and carried on until they saw a sign for a footpath leading into a wooded area. They continued walking in a happy, comfortable silence for a while. The footpath waned a little and then joined a slightly bigger track that ran by a long, dry-stone wall.

"This is a long trail…some kind of National Trust beauty thing. I saw it on one of the maps. It might be nice to follow it."

"The day is ours. We've got water and Pop-Tarts in our bags. Why not?"

The sun rose higher in the sky. When Wren had suggested this, she'd imagined she and Robyn would be gabbing non-stop, but they were both relishing the scenery, the sun and the silence. It felt like a vacation. Just one day where nothing was expected of them.

"How far do you think we've come? Is there a distance thing on that compass of yours?"

Wren gave Robyn a look. "A compass is nothing more than a needle that points to the magnetic north. That's it, Bobbi."

"Okay, brainiac, I was only asking."

"I'd guess we've come about three miles, maybe a bit more."

They carried on walking for a while longer before Wren stopped suddenly. "What is it?" Robyn asked, urgently.

Wren put down her javelin and slid the rucksack from her shoulders. She pulled out a pair of binoculars and focussed. There was a figure leant up against the wall ahead.

"Get ready with your bow," Wren said, and Robyn immediately nocked an arrow. "I think there's an infected up ahead, but it's acting weird. It's just leaning against the wall."

"What makes you think it's a zombie and not a person?"

"It's covered in blood, for a start and—oh my god. I think it's Strand."

"What? How can you tell?"

"His arm's bandaged where I shot him." Wren placed the binoculars back in the rucksack and both sisters began to jog towards the figure.

"He must be dead already. If he was one of those things, he would have been on his feet and heading towards us long before now."

"Can't afford to take any risks," Wren said as the pair of them slowed down.

They stopped twenty metres back. Robyn pulled back her bowstring again, ready, and Wren raised her javelin, but still, the figure did not stir. Its skin was pallid, but there was a slight pink hue to it. "I don't think he's dead," Robyn said.

"Strand! Strand!" Wren called.

Strand slowly lifted his head and turned towards them. There was a sad and agonised look on his face, but suddenly it lifted as he saw the two girls.

"Girls," he said in little more than a whisper.

They continued to hold their weapons on him from a few feet back. "What happened to you?" Wren asked.

He slowly looked down at his shirt and saw blood stains from where he had battled with the creatures. There was more blood as the welts from his neck had opened up and still more from the wound on his arm. "I must look like some sight. One of those things tore into me," he said. His mouth was dry and Wren put down her javelin and rucksack, pulling out a bottle of water.

She walked towards Strand and knelt down beside him. "Here drink this," she said, about to hand him the bottle.

"No!" he replied abruptly, cupping his hands instead.

Wren poured water into them and he drank thirstily. "So did it get Cadmore, too?"

"No. Listen...I don't have long. I was heading back to the Manor. I prayed—believe that if you will—I prayed for the strength to get back there, but I couldn't...and then he sends me you two."

"Erm...okay," Robyn said. "Get back why?"

"Warning. I...I was stupid. I shouldn't have...I should have tried to help Georgie and Stevenson. I was a..."

"You were an arse!" Robyn said, finally lowering her bow.

Strand laughed until he fell into a coughing fit. When he'd calmed down again, he looked towards Robyn. "Yes, I was."

"I'm sorry I shot you," Wren said, screwing the top back on the bottle.

"Don't be. I deserved it. Listen to me those men...the ones you talked about...Loch Uig." He closed his eyes for a moment as speaking and thinking became harder. He let out a breath, opened his eyes, and continued. "We went there."

Wren and Robyn looked at one another. "You went there?" Wren asked.

"Cadmore...Cadmore's one of them now."

"What? You're not making sense," Wren said.

Strand's hand shot out and grabbed Wren's wrist. "Listen to me. They're monsters...what they do there...they'll bring your worst nightmares with them...when they come...when they come to the Manor." He released his grip and his eyes closed again. "You need to get out," he whispered. "They're coming."

"Strand! Strand!" Wren shouted shaking his arm.

"I was going back...going back to warn you all.... You need to get out."

"They're building defences, they've got guns, they've got the walls," Robyn began.

"You don't understand. It's a proper army...hundreds...and hundreds...they've got guns, grenades, mortars...stuff you wouldn't believe...and Cadmore's told them everything...everything about the place. You need to get out. What they do...what they do in that place...the women...you need to get out." His eyelids fluttered.

"Strand...Strand!" Wren said.

His face had lost all its colour now and he struggled to keep his eyes open. "Tell them I'm sorry...tell them."

"I will," Wren replied.

"I need you to...do something."

"What?"

"Kill me, Wren. Now."

Wren immediately let go of his arm and stood up. "No. Don't ask me that."

Strand looked at her for a moment and smiled. He lifted his wounded arm. "You don't want to finish the job?" The smile disappeared from his face. "I don't want to turn into one of those things...please."

"There's a difference. There's a difference between killing the living and killing the dead," Wren said.

Strand swallowed, "Plea—" the arrow went straight through his head and Wren gasped.

She turned to look at her sister. The bowstring was still vibrating and Robyn's eyes were still lined up with the sight window.

"God, Bobbi."

"He was going to turn. He was as good as dead."

Wren looked back towards Strand. His head had dropped to one side and blood trickled from the entry wound made by the arrow. "He tried to make it back to warn everyone. I was wrong about him."

"Naa, he was a tosser...but he wasn't a monster. Looks like we're heading back to the Manor then," Robyn said, handing Wren her javelin.

Wren looked down the footpath and to the woods beyond. "So much for our day out."

16

Fry puffed on his cigar and bored holes through TJ with his blue, laser beam eyes. "You sure you think you're ready for this?" he growled in his rich, Glaswegian accent.

TJ showed Fry his arm, clenched and unclenched his fist multiple times, a small grimace appeared briefly on his face, but he tried to mask it with a smile. "It's them...I know it's them. That little bitch who nearly killed me."

"Let me get this straight. You're wanting to take an army down there for revenge?" Fry glared at TJ.

"No. No, definitely not. This is business. That's all it's ever about. She's just the icing on the cake. This place is ripe, Fry...ripe for the picking."

"Are you sure you don't want to rest a couple more days at least?"

"I promised you that I would get this place on track, bring in supplies, weapons, entertainment for the men. I said I'd train lieutenants you could rely on for the day that—" he stopped suddenly as Fry's eyes narrowed. Would TJ speak the unspeakable? Fry and he had spoken about the way The Don was running things. It had all been hypothetical, but TJ knew there was more to it. Fry had spoken at length about how things were getting worse with the Don and his idiot daughter, Lorelei. He spoke about what would be needed to run this place properly—if one day it was Fry and not the Don in charge. But that had all been hypothetical…of course.

"You were saying?"

"Erm…look. That place has it all. It would be a huge win for us...for you."

Fry picked his glass of whisky up from the table and took a drink, then took another long puff on his cigar. The blue smoke drifted further across the table like ink in water, dying everything in its path. Fry continued to stare at TJ, then suddenly, he felt exploring fingers from behind him creep over his shoulders to his chest. "Come on, Daddy, you've got a date, remember?" said a velvety voice.

"Ahhh Juliet. My sweet Juliet. I'm working here, darlin'," Fry said, smiling.

"I erm...so, am I okay to head out, boss?" TJ asked, desperate to escape a situation that was clearly becoming more intimate by the second.

Fry roused momentarily from his lustful thoughts and fixed his glare on TJ once more. "No. Not this time. I'm going to send Burwell."

"What?" TJ said, standing up.

"Oh TJ, honey, calm yourself down," Juliet said.

"Believe me, I understand wanting revenge, but you'll get your chance. When those itsy bitsy little girls are back here, you can get all the revenge you want. But you're so important to this place. You going out there while you're still recovering wouldn't be a smart move, now would it?"

TJ glared at her. This had been her, influencing Fry's decision. "Boss I'm—"

"Juliet's right, we need you back to fitness."

"Then let's wait a few days then. I can—"

"I said it's been decided," Fry said, giving TJ a stare.

Juliet picked up Fry's glass and took a long, sensual gulp, draining it. "Be a sweetheart, TJ. Fill me up before you go," she said, sliding the glass across the table.

"Erm...yeah...sure...no problem." TJ stifled his rage for a moment and took the glass across to the bar. He half-filled it before taking it back to the table and sliding it towards Fry and Juliet who had now lost interest in him completely. "Right then. I'll be heading out."

Juliet wrapped her lips around Fry's. He closed his eyes, losing himself in the moment, but Juliet kept hers wide open and cast them in TJ's direction. He was not sure what the look she gave him meant, but as he walked out of the room, a shiver ran down his spine.

*

"Can we stop for just a minute?" Robyn said, bending over and placing her hands on her thighs for support.

"You do understand what's going on here, don't you?"

"Of course I understand. I just need to catch my breath. We can't all be medal-winning athletes, sister dearest."

"I don't want to fight about it, I'm just saying."

"Yeah…'course you are."

"Bobbi, don't be like that. I'm just saying…"

"Too many Pop-Tarts. I'm going to have to go on a diet."

"Well, now that you mention it…. Are you okay? Seriously?"

"What do you mean?" Robyn asked straightening up.

"What you did. What you did to Strand."

"He was going to turn. I might not have liked the guy, but he tried to do the right thing in the end, and he asked us to do the right thing too. You know what was coming for him."

"Yeah…it's just I still struggle."

"I suppose that's good…you know, that we don't get used to it."

"I'm not so sure," Wren said, looking back to the direction of travel.

"Look, if that army's as big and as well-armed as Strand said, we've only got one option. We need to get everybody out. Take our chances on the outside."

"The outside? The outside where? There are sick and old people. What will they do?"

"What I'm going to say sounds pretty heartless, but remember what we promised each other."

"Yeah...I don't suppose we can be responsible for everyone."

Robyn picked up her bow again. "Ready?" she asked.

"Ready," Wren replied, and they started running again.

They ran without pause, through the pain and the fatigue. With each metre they travelled, with each second that passed, the urgency grew. Finally, they began to recognise their surroundings, and the woodland gave way to the village. The road was deathly quiet, the pounding of their feet against the tarmac was the only sound either of them could hear.

"Who goes there?" Dan asked in a jokey voice as the two sisters reached the gate. He was visible from the waist up as he looked down at them from the top of the wall. "How do you like my new guard platform?" he asked, springing up and down a little.

"Yeah...great...let us in, Dan," Robyn said, trying to catch her breath.

"What's the password?"

"Password...let me see. How about, there's a huge army heading this way with guns, mortars and grenades. Is that it? Is that the bloody password?"

The cocksure smile suddenly disappeared from Dan's face. "W—what?"

"You heard me," Robyn replied.

"Open it up," he called down to one of the other guards and a second later, the bolts squeaked and the sturdy gates glided inwards.

Robyn and Wren walked in and in a flash, Dan was there with them. He turned to one of the other men. "Grafton, take over," he said, signalling to the platform.

Wren and Robyn stood there for a moment, looking around the grounds. The new platform was one of two, either side of the gate. They looked over to Ed's workshop and a small team was working on erecting more. The gardens were a hive of activity, people were getting on with the usual weeding and planting, but always with one eye on the thirty or so trainees in the new militia. Georgie and Stevenson each headed a group. For the time being, they were not using any ammunition, they were just getting used to the feel of the rifles, how to load, how to aim, but it was still a cause for excitement in a village where, up until a few weeks ago, nothing had ever happened.

Robyn and Wren went straight across to Georgie, with Dan behind them. "We need to talk," Wren said quietly.

"I should be done in another ten minutes or so," Georgie said smiling.

"No, we need to talk now," Robyn insisted.

Georgie handed the rifle back to the recruit she had been helping and guided the two girls to one side, noticing the concerned look on Dan's face. "What's this about?"

"We need to speak to Stevenson too...away from here," Wren said, looking up to see a multitude of curious faces staring in her direction.

"I'll go get him," Dan said, as Robyn, Wren and Georgie walked up the steps to the Manor. The entrance hall was empty, but the three of them headed towards the huge dining room. When Dan and Stevenson joined them, Robyn closed the doors to make sure their conversation could not be overheard.

"What's all this about?" Stevenson asked.

"We came across Strand?" Wren said.

"What?" Georgie asked. "What was he doing?"

"He was trying to get back here to warn us."

"Warn us? About what?"

"Him and Cadmore ended up in Loch Uig. He said the place was worse than we could imagine. He said the army was huge and well equipped and they were going to be heading here. Cadmore had given them every last detail about the Manor, about Cromore," Wren said.

"Just like Strand to blame someone else...I bet he gave them plenty," Dan said.

"No. He was being totally honest with us," Robyn said.

"No offence, but I know him better than you."

"No doubt, but he had nothing to lose. He'd been attacked by one of the infected. He didn't have long left; he knew he was going to die. He told us we had to get back here and warn everyone. We had to evacuate while we still had chance."

"Evacuate? Screw that," Georgie said. "They want to try coming here we're going to give them a fight to remember."

"If they come here, we'll be destroyed," Wren replied. "They've got mortars, grenades and hundreds and hundreds of men."

The defiant look on Georgie's face vanished. Stevenson looked out of the window. "But there's no way we can get out of here. We've got old people, children. There's nowhere for us to go. What do we do? Travel around like a bunch of desperate refugees until we run out of fuel? Who's to say they wouldn't find us anyway?"

"We could go cross-country," Dan said. "Leave the vehicles...go where vehicles can't. Live like the Highlanders used to...build huts and stuff."

"Oh yeah. How do you think Mrs Macmanus would like the winter in a hut? Or Mr Gunn? Or the small children? They'd freeze...they'd starve," Georgie said.

"What's the answer then?" Dan asked.

"I don't know, Dan. All this is coming at me just the same as it is to you. I need time to think," Georgie said.

Stevenson pulled a chair out from underneath the long thick wooded dining table and slumped down. "Did Strand say when?"

"No...it was just…y'know...he thought it was going to happen quick."

"Oh man! We're screwed. We're royally screwed," Dan said.

"Dan. Stop that. People look to you...they look to us. We need to be strong," Stevenson replied.

"Okay...first thing we need to do is get the North barricade up and running again. At least that'll give us a few minutes' warning," Georgie said, suddenly taking charge again. "Dan, get onto it, and for the time being, you don't say a word to anyone. We just say that Wren and Robyn found a few infected while they were out and we're taking precautions."

"Me? You want me to man it by myself?"

"I'm not asking you to fight them by yourself! I'm just asking you to be a lookout. Take something fast, take a walkie-talkie and the first sign of anything, you radio to us and get back here."

"Got it," he said, heading out of the room and closing the door behind him.

Wren went over to one of the windows and looked out. She watched the people's faces as Dan re-emerged and gave instructions to one of the other guards. "It would not be long before rumours began to circulate and nerves started to jangle. Wren looked back to the table to see Georgie had sat down too, now. Robyn slid the rucksack from her back and placed it next to Wren's by the door. They had been in such a rush to speak to Georgie and Stevenson that they had not even dropped their weapons off in their quarters. They had simply leaned them against the wall, a constant reminder that there would never be a true rest for them, of the taking up of arms to survive...again.

"Should we not put a lookout on the southerly approach too?" Wren asked.

"Coming through Aberfeldy is the most direct route from Loch Uig. Plus, to the south, there are hundreds of infected. They don't seem to have made their way back here, so when Banks lured them away with that lorry fire, they stayed there or thereabouts, I'm guessing." Wren walked over to the table and sat down at the end. She had a distant, almost glazed look on her face.

"We don't have a choice," Georgie said. "We can't evacuate. All the preparations we've been making have been to fortify this place in case we needed to go to war. Looks like that's going to happen. Live or die, we don't have a choice; we just have to put up the good fight and hope."

"Erm...no offence, but I hope you're going to give that lot out there a better speech," Robyn said.

"Maybe we should try and get the kids and old folks out of here. Maybe we could—" Stevenson began.

"I've got it," Wren said, slapping her hand down on the table.

"You've got what?" Georgie asked.

"I've got how we can win this."

"How?"

"Fire!"

17

There was no hint of a smile on Wren's face as she spoke the word and it echoed around the room.

"And there we have it. Wren's solution to all life's problems," Robyn said, slumping onto a chair. "Come on then, brainiac, enlighten us. How is burning this place down going to help us?"

"Not here," Wren said, as if the idea was still forming in her head.

"Erm...what are you thinking, Wren?" Georgie asked.

"Okay...this'll need fine-tuning, but here goes. There's one main road in Aberfeldy that could give them access to Cromore, yes?"

"Right," Stevenson replied.

"So, we strand them."

"What?"

"Strand them? How do you mean?"

"We immobilise them. I'm guessing it's going to be a big convoy, so we immobilise them and block them in. Then we send up smoke signals and get every infected in a ten-mile radius to descend on them," Wren said.

"And how do we immobilise them?" Georgie asked.

"I haven't figured that out yet."

"No...course you haven't. The fire thing came to you right away, but the little details—they're a bit harder, aren't they?" Robyn snarked.

"This might actually work," Stevenson said.

"We could lose a lot of people, even if we do manage to pull it off," Georgie said.

"No," Wren replied. "This won't work with a lot of people. It's got to be a small guerrilla team...a surprise attack. Then, while they're wondering what the hell has happened, the team makes their escape."

"So, if the plan's to attract every zombie in the area, how do they escape?" Georgie asked.

"Cross-country," Wren replied.

"Oh...I seeeee," Robyn said. "So, the guerrilla force disables this huge army, sets fire to the town, then goes on a little jog through zombie-infested countryside to finish off the day. Yeah, that sounds brilliant. Great plan. Count me in."

"I thought you'd like it," Wren said smiling.

"Okay, just to be clear, I was being sarcastic," Robyn replied.

"Well duh!"

"It could work. Seriously...I think it's the best option we've got. I think I know how to make it work, too," Stevenson said.

"Go on," Georgie replied.

"We block off the side streets and put a big blockade in place on the main street. Then take out the last couple of vehicles, trapping the ones in the middle," Stevenson said excitedly.

"How?" Georgie asked.

"I'm going to see Ed. We'll need a few vehicles and the 7.5-tonner; we're going to lose that, I'm afraid. I'll need about ten men, ladders, diesel. We've got no idea when this army will come; they could catch us out before we get a chance to do this, so we've got to start moving." He headed to the door and left, leaving Georgie, Wren and Robyn just looking at each other.

"What just happened?" Robyn said.

"Looks like we're taking a trip," Wren replied.

"We?" said Robyn.

"Trust me, for this to work, they're going to need us."

Robyn let out a deflated sigh. "I hate your plans."

"Sorry, sis," Wren replied before turning to Georgie. "You should stay here in case it doesn't work."

"Stuff that. If it doesn't work we're all goners anyway. If there's a fight to be had, I'm in."

Wren looked Georgie in the eyes. "There's going to be a fight, alright. The fight of our lives."

18

Georgie called the entire population of the Manor to an emergency meeting. She relayed to them what Strand had said, and an electrifying panic began to bristle around the place. Frantic looks and feverish questions sprang from all over the huge dining room.

"Look, I've told you everything we know. We've got a plan; a few of us are heading to Aberfeldy. If the plan works, we'll be able to cut them off there," she said, trying to relieve some of the tension.

"And if it doesn't?" asked a worried-looking woman holding on to her baby.

"Then the rest of the guards and the militia here will go back to plan A. Listen, we've got guard towers, and all kinds of defences have been built for this place. We can put up a stand here; that's what we've been doing these last days: fortifying this place."

"So if it's such a fortress, why leave it? Why go to Aberfeldy?" a man from the crowd asked.

"Because we want to stack the odds in our favour, avoid confrontation on our turf, if we can. Listen. We can talk about this until the cows come home, but the time for talking is over. Dan's going to be in charge until we get back. If you need anything, see him." Questions and murmurs continued to circulate around the dining room, but Georgie ignored them. She jumped down from the table and headed out. Her family were waiting outside the room. She had not wanted Pippa to be there, but she had already explained the situation to her mother and father.

"Be careful, sweet pea," Steven said.

Tears appeared in Patricia's eyes. "I…"

"Love you, Mum," Georgie said before kneeling down and flinging her arms around Pippa. "You be good for your Gran and Grandad, I'll see you soon," she said, embracing the girl tightly, and giving her a big kiss. She stood back up, looked again at her mum and dad and headed towards the entrance. She knew that if she looked back or if she thought about what she was doing, in all likelihood, she would back out. So Georgie kept going. She walked through the doors and out into the open.

There was a procession of vehicles all with their engines running. When Georgie climbed into the passenger seat of the Land Rover that was parked directly behind the 7.5-tonne truck, the gates swung open and the convoy began to move.

Georgie turned and looked towards the doors of the Manor. Her mum, dad and daughter had assembled on the top step to watch the procession, and that image was the final straw, as tears began to roll down Georgie's face.

The Land Rover headed through the gate, and the driver stopped and rolled down the window. Dan leaned inside. "Good luck, guys, I'll keep things in order until you get back," he said with a smile that even he didn't believe. He stood up and tapped his hand on the roof as the vehicle moved off once again.

"Are you okay?" Wren asked, leaning forward from the back seat to put a comforting hand on Georgie's shoulder.

"No…but we've got a job to do."

It was only a few short miles to Aberfeldy, but knowing what they were heading into made it seem like a trek to the other side of the world. All the doubts, all the apprehension...the prospect that they could be too late and they would meet the giant army already heading to Cromore...it all filled them with a sickening dread. Each bend in the road made, shredded their nerves a little more.

The Land Rover came to a stop as the truck turned right onto a farm road. "What's happening?" Robyn asked.

The driver turned around in his seat to look at them. "Well, if all goes to plan, this road is going to be swarming with the dead. The farm is our rendezvous point. There will be half a dozen quad bikes there waiting for us. Not perfect, and we're going to have to share, but it beats walking."

"Sweet! I know my sister was looking forward to making me run a few miles, but I much prefer that plan," Robyn said.

"Yeah, well, that's assuming we don't all die horribly before then," he said smiling and turning around to the direction of travel once more.

"Just for the record, you might want to work on your whole positive visualisation thing. I don't think it's working for you," Robyn said.

"Duly noted," the driver said, making eye contact with Robyn in the rearview mirror.

The next few minutes passed in silence, but when the truck reappeared on the main road, the journey was underway again. They were not travelling long before they arrived in the now familiar town centre.

The procession of vehicles pulled up and parked on the main street. Paranoia grew in all the occupants as they waited. Any minute...any second...that giant army could be arriving, foiling their plans before they even had a chance to put them into motion.

Stevenson pulled the handbrake on and climbed out of the truck. He looked around, turning a full three hundred and sixty degrees. He scanned the area for anything out of place, looking up at the windows, the rooftops, looking down the side streets. He walked along the line of vehicles to a compact, sporty-looking Volkswagen. The driver rolled the window down.

"Remember what I said to you. Find a good vantage point. The second you see them, radio in, then get back here as fast as you possibly can." He extended his hand and the driver grasped it with an iron grip. "Good luck, Davey."

"Good luck, Stevo," he replied before pulling out of line and disappearing up the main street.

Stevenson watched him go and unclipped the radio from his belt. "Davey, remember to do a radio check when you get there. Over."

"Will do. Over and out," came the crackly response.

Stevenson replaced the radio on his belt and signalled for the rest of the team to get out of their cars. They assembled in a semi-circle around him. "Okay, listen up. We need to get this done as quickly as possible because we've got no idea when we're going to get interrupted. This street—this is the only street we're interested in." He walked down the line to where the last car had parked and his audience all followed. "This is the blockade," he said, waving both his hands across the street. The truck is going to be parked in line with this alley. Another car is going to be parked in front of it, two more on the other side, then we'll pile what we can on top and behind, just leaving enough of a gap for the infected to get through."

"What about the side streets?" Wren asked.

"We're going to block all three of them off with the other vehicles; we'll park them horizontally across as well. Robyn, you're key to us getting those side streets impassable." He looked up to the third-floor window of one of the Victorian buildings. The lower floor was a long-defunct Chinese takeaway, but floors two and three were offices. "You reckon you can get one of your arrows through a rolled down car window at that distance?"

"'Course. Erm…why?"

"'Cos the cars are going to be doused in diesel. Your arrows are going to be lit, and these side streets aren't just going to be barricaded, they're going to be on fire, too," Stevenson said.

"Course they are," Robyn replied, giving her sister a look.

"Right," Stevenson said, turning to the rest of them, "We don't know how big the convoy is, so for the time being, we can't determine where we need to disable the last vehicle. That's going to be the riskiest job, and I wouldn't ask anybody to do what I'm not prepared to do myself, so that's going to be down to me."

"How are you intending to disable the vehicles?" Wren asked.

"We've got two milk crates full of Molotov Cocktails stuffed with nails and screws," Stevenson said, heading to the back of the truck, removing one of the crates and placing it down in front of the group. "I can't say Ed was too happy about me raiding his supplies," he laughed quietly. "The front vehicle and the back vehicle are the keys to all this." Stevenson pointed to the third-floor window of the building that was level with where the first vehicle would pull up in front of the blockade. "Georgie, I want you up there. Light them then throw them down towards the wheels. Jason…" he said, turning towards another member of the group. "You'll be in the alley with the truck parked at the end. We'll open up the back where there's going to be a lot of diesel, some old tyres—all sorts of crap. I want you to light it up. The smoke's going to be seen for miles."

"What happens then? What happens when we've stopped the convoy and started the fire?" Wren asked.

"We get out as fast as we can?" Georgie said. "These men aren't just going to sit back and let us do all this. The first sign of trouble, I'm guessing they'll be out of the vehicles, charging into the buildings and down the alleys trying to get to us before we do more damage. That's why the second we've done what we need to do, we get out. The ladders are going to be set up at the back of the buildings. The alleys to the back are going to be blockaded and on fire. It won't stop them for good, but it will hopefully delay them long enough for us to make our escape."

"That's something else I forgot to mention," Stevenson said. "For those of you in the buildings, make sure the stairwells are blocked. Make sure there are plenty of obstacles because we don't want them getting to you before you've had the chance to make it to the ladders."

"What are you wanting me to do?" Wren asked.

"I want you and Strauss on bodyguard duty. Robyn really is key to all of this. Those side streets lighting up will be—"

Everyone immediately looked towards Stevenson as he stopped talking in mid-sentence. It was only when he fell forward and crashed to the ground that they realised what that soft sound...that pfft had actually been. They looked at his body on the floor, they looked at the hole in the back of his head as blood began to gush from it and suddenly, they heard another pfft, and Jason crumpled to the floor.

They all hit the ground as another bullet shattered the glass of the abandoned takeaway. A fourth bullet entered the front passenger side tyre of the minibus and for a brief moment, the only sound was the dull whistle of air escaping before a booming voice echoed down the street.

"There doesn't need to be any more killing. If you surrender your weapons now and come out with your hands raised, my snipers will stand down. You are massively outnumbered and escape is impossible." As soon as the voice stopped talking, the group heard engines, and seconds later, brakes squealed from multiple directions as the main street and the side streets were blockaded by several vehicles.

"Oh shit!" Georgie said. "They stole our plan."

"We're going to have to surrender," Moretti said.

"The second you step out, you'll be dead," Wren said.

"We don't know that. They could easily take us all out right now. If they've got grenades, like Strand said they had, it would be easy, so why don't they do that? No...I say—"

"You do what you want," Robyn interrupted, "but my sister's right. The second we go out there, you'll be dead and Georgie, myself and Wren will be taken as prizes, so we're not going anywhere. I'd rather die right here."

Georgie grabbed the radio from her belt. "Davey...Davey can you hear me. Over?"

The radio crackled, "Davey can't make it to the radio right now, but if you'd like to leave a message, he'll get back to you as soon as he can." It was the same voice who had shouted the demands down the street. "It was a good plan...placing a lookout a little way out of town...shame we didn't think of it...oh wait a second, we did. Can't believe the luck, though. This was only a stopover for us before we headed to your mansion. To get your whole strike force like this...let's just say my bosses are going to be very happy. Now drop your weapons and come on out before I have to start playing nasty."

They all looked at the radio as it fell silent again. "We need to get down the alleys, out of the town, to the farm. If we can get to the quad bikes and back to the Manor, at least we can try and put up a defence there."

"A defence?" Moretti said. "Are you mad?"

"There aren't any other options. If we head down the alleys, we can get to the woodland at the back then at least—"

"Don't shoot!" Moretti said, standing up. "I'm surrendering."

"Moretti! Get down, you fool," Georgie said, but it was too late. Moretti walked from behind the cover of the

145

car with his hands up. When he got out into the open and nobody took a shot at him, the other seven men did the same thing, leaving Wren, Robyn and Georgie still taking cover behind the vehicle.

"Bloody idiots," Georgie spat.

"Bloody cowards, more like," Robyn said.

Georgie removed the rifle from her shoulder and placed it on the ground. She leaned forward and pulled Stevenson's body towards her. She grabbed his pistol and the spare magazines from his pockets. "If we're making a run for it, I don't want to be lugging that thing with me, and somebody misplaced my gun," she said, looking at Wren.

"I see some of you want to do this the hard way then," the voice boomed down the road once more.

"I left my javelin in the car," Wren said, sliding the rucksack from her shoulders. She crawled forward a little, making sure she stayed out of the line of sight of the enemy. Her left hand clutched the handle of the bottle crate and she dragged it across the ground towards them. Wren removed her two pistol crossbows from her backpack and carefully placed two of the Molotov cocktails upright in the mesh side pockets. She loaded the crossbows and placed them down in front of her.

"Erm...mind letting us in on the plan, sis?" Robyn said.

"We need to create a little mayhem to try and make it to the alley," she replied, pulling two more nail bombs from the crate. She pulled a lighter from her pocket.

"Hang on a second. If this is going to be our last hurrah, we should make it a big one," Georgie said, pulling more cocktails from the crate and lining them up in front of the three of them.

Multiple gunshots sounded, and Wren peeked over the bonnet of the car to see the seven men who had surrendered collapse to the ground. "idiots," she said, shaking her head.

"Right. I've had enough of this shit. Move in," shouted the voice.

Wren and Georgie lit the cotton wool fuses to the eight bottles on the curb, and all three of them watched for just a moment, mentally preparing themselves for the fight that was coming. "If this is it, I just want to say, it's been a real pleasure knowing you girls."

"This is like Dad's favourite film, Butch Cassidy and the Sundance Kid, y'know at the end where—"

"I swear to god I'm going to slap you if you finish that sentence," Robyn said.

Wren took the first bottle, and while still crouching low, flung it at the truck. The bottle exploded against the windscreen, instantly setting fire to the cab and showering the vehicle in front and the surrounding area in flaming nails. Georgie took another bottle and threw it in the other direction, setting fire to the minibus at the rear of the convoy. Robyn took a third bottle and chucked it into the abandoned takeaway, whose window had already been shattered. There was a bright and powerful explosion as the bottle burst into flames. Fiery nails shot into the walls and within seconds the fire caught, while the girls disposed of the other bottles. Two shattered on the pavement: one towards the rear of their convoy, one towards the front. One more lit another of the vehicles up, and the final two, as nobody wanted to break cover from the concealment of the car they crouched behind, were thrown blind.

One of them smashed on the road, causing a small eruption of nails to arc in various directions—but nowhere near anybody or anything. The second landed in front of a group of Loch Uig troops and there was a sudden volley of agonised screams as burning nails entered bone, glass sliced through flesh, and flames began to devour clothing. Shrieks of pain filled the air over the growing sound of the crackle of the fires.

Georgie looked at both girls. "Three, two, one, NOW!!!"

19

The man next to Burwell fired as the women broke free, and Burwell immediately lashed out. The smoke from the burning vehicles and building already impaired the chance to get a clear shot and Burwell had issued strict instructions for the women to be taken unharmed.

The rifle flew out of the man's hands and he collapsed to the floor as the other troops around were suddenly taken aback by the show of force from Burwell.

"I told you. They need to be taken alive." he almost spat the words.

The man on the floor was still stunned by the force of the blow. "But they're—"

"No buts. Fry gave me this mission. TJ told me there'd be trouble if females were hurt. He's got a particular interest in one of them."

"We could just say they got caught in crossfire."

"Yeah, like some snake here wouldn't tell him what actually happened and then I'm history." He turned to look at the other men. "What the hell are you just standing around for!? Get after them!" he shouted. "Leg shots if you have to. Hobble them, stop them, but don't kill them." All the men began to charge towards where the three women had disappeared, and Burwell turned to the armour-plated bus behind him. He climbed on board and looked down the aisle to see forty heavily armed men awaiting instructions. Burwell turned towards the driver, pulling a map from his pocket.

"Where do you want us?" the driver asked.

About a mile south there's a farm. Go there. You stay put with a dozen men while the rest of them head here on foot. Somewhere in between there and meeting up with the rest of the men coming from here, we're going to get these girls. I don't want any mistakes. I want all this to run smoothly, I don't want anyone moaning to TJ or Fry that 'we could have done this' or 'that could have been done.' You understand me?"

The driver nodded. "Sure thing."

Burwell climbed back down from the bus and slapped the side. The door closed and the bus moved away. He watched it travel down the street, giving the burning convoy a wide berth. It turned left and then it was gone.

"Right! I want my squad to stay here with me. The rest of you, I want you to head after those girls," he said, looking around. For a moment, nobody moved. "I want them found. We've got over three hundred men here; if we can't find three women, there'll be a price to pay." The men moved out straight away, and Burwell pulled the guard, who was still on the ground, to his feet. The man wiped blood from his mouth.

"I'm sorry. I was…out of line. I just didn't want them to get away," the man said. Burwell just looked at him. "We don't know it was the girl that TJ was after."

Burwell turned towards the rest of his men. "Spread out, just in case they try and double back or something. Keep your eyes peeled." Burwell looked at the man still wiping blood from his mouth. He tapped the binoculars that were strapped around his chest. "TJ described that girl I saw down to her pert little cheeks. That new bloke, Cadmore, told him she went everywhere with her sister. Described her too. Those are the girls, alright, and I'm going to make sure they're wrapped up in a nice little bow for TJ before the end of the day."

*

Robyn, Wren and Georgie all spluttered as they ran down the narrow alley to the small parking bay at the back of the shops. They did not pause as the three of them leapt over the knee-high stone wall and sprinted down the embankment, leapfrogging the narrow stream before heading up the wooded incline. As they passed the first few trees, shouts and calls followed them into the woods. The chase was on.

Wren turned to see dozens of men appearing from the mouths of the alleys. "Don't look back, just run," she said.

The three women clung onto their weapons in vice-like grips. "I really don't want to see what's behind us, so no fear there," Georgie replied.

"And remember, those lowlifes aren't the only thing we need to be looking out for. That smoke will be starting to rise high. Any zombie with a pair of eyes will be headed in this direction," Wren said.

"Thanks, sis. I wasn't scared enough already; you've really put my mind at ease," Robyn said.

A voice shouted from behind them: "Col, you head that way. Seb, veer right, you see anything—radio."

"Crap, they don't sound that far behind," Georgie only half-whispered.

"Don't think about it—just keep going," Wren said, hurdling a tree stump.

They'd been running for a few minutes when a man's scream cut through the mossy air. "My ankle…my bloody ankle!"

Rather than bringing the three women relief that one of them had been injured, the sound made them concentrate even more on where they were running. One stupid mistake and it was all over.

The trees and shrubbery gradually began to thin. "It won't be long before we hit the farm," Georgie said. "I'll be glad to climb onto one of the quads and—"

Wren put her hand up to silence her and put her other arm out to stop her sister. Robyn was about to ask what was going on when she heard it too. Her eyes widened as voices approached them from in front. Wren looked around for a good hiding place for the three of them, but there was nothing. Then her eyes focussed on an ancient-looking oak up ahead. She pointed upwards. Robyn and Georgie immediately understood what she meant.

Wren slid her rucksack off and placed her bows inside. Georgie holstered her pistol in the back of her jeans, and Robyn hooked her bow onto her rucksack as the three of them began to climb; no talk, no hesitation. The voices were getting closer and they all knew what was at stake.

They hid, frozen, in the foliage, midway up, as a gang of six men approached. The group stopped suddenly in their tracks directly beneath the tree. Robyn, Wren and Georgie held their breath.

"What's that?" one of the men asked.

"Come out slowly," said another, raising his rifle.

"What do you think you're doing? Do I look like a fifteen-year-old girl to you." said the leader of another group of men as they emerged out of the trees.

"More like a twenty stone blob of lard."

"You're a funny man, Baz. See if you're laughing when our bollocks get nailed to a tree 'cos we've lost these women. They must have got past you."

"Probably doubled back and got past you, more like," Baz replied.

"Anybody seen any sign?" the other man said, hitting the talk button on the radio.

Multiple replies came through, all of them negative. "Well, they were definitely coming here. Burwell told us to stake out the farm. There's a bunch of quads there, all fuelled up and ready to go," Baz said.

"Right. We'll retrace our steps to town; you head back to the farm. They've got to be around here somewhere." He brought the handheld radio back up to his mouth and hit the talk button. "Everyone who came from the town, make your way to the edge of the woodland then retrace your steps," he said before leading his group back towards Aberfeldy.

The six men beneath the tree scanned the area one last time. "Here puss, puss, puss," Baz said and the other five laughed. "I don't care about Burwell being hacked off with us, but TJ will have our heads if we don't find those girls." They turned and slowly walked back in the direction of the farm, gradually spreading out wider. When silence had befallen the area once again, Robyn, Wren and Georgie let out long breaths as they continued to cling to the tree like koala bears hugging a eucalyptus.

"We're trapped," Wren said.

"Wow. You figured that out by yourself?" Robyn replied.

"Okay...no way can we head back to town. We're going to have to see what's waiting at the farm," Georgie said.

"What, you mean other than a load of heavily armed men?" Robyn asked.

"Wouldn't it make more sense to head east, forget about the quads, and circumnavigate the whole place?"

"Erm east? Circumnavigate? Hello, speaky the English?" Robyn said.

Wren let out a sigh and pointed. "We walk that way until we're well past the farm, then turn right and head back to the Manor."

"Thank you. Wasn't too hard, was it?" Robyn said.

"It's worth a try, I suppose. There's nothing to say we won't run into them looking for us though," Georgie replied.

"We'll run into fewer of them than we will at the farm."

"True enough. Okay, let's try," Georgie said, climbing down. She hit the ground, quickly followed by Robyn.

The strap from Wren's rucksack got caught around a branch and she had to slip it from her shoulders to get it free. She untangled the strap and was about to hoist it back on and climb down when she heard the laughter of two men. "Well, well, well, look what we've got here," said one of them.

"Baz, guess what we've found," the other one said, hitting the talk button on the radio. "It's more or less in the same spot we met the others a few minutes ago."

"Nice work," Baz replied. "Hold your positions, we'll be there in a minute."

"Funny, I was just cursing him, asking what the point was of doubling back to the town. I suppose that's why I'm not the boss," the first man said, making the other laugh.

"Two lookers, these, Hoggy. Looks like we've got our entertainment sorted out for the journey back," and both men laughed again.

"Where's the other one?" the first demanded.

"I...I don't know. We got split up," Georgie said.

"Oh well, two's better than none."

A few seconds passed and more men could be heard approaching in the distance. There were laughs and shouts that got louder by the second.

"I reckon TJ's going to be happy with you and me; there'll be a bonus in this for—" The bolt entered his forehead and a single stream of blood trickled down onto his nose. It dripped off the tip and onto his chin before his whole body collapsed backwards.

By the time the second man had grasped what was happening, a bolt had burrowed down diagonally through his right temple. Wren's rucksack dropped to the ground at the same time as he did. A split second later, Wren was down, too. She grabbed a handful of bolts and put them in her pocket, swung the rucksack back onto her shoulder, and the three women began to head east as fast as they could.

"Oh no!" Georgie said, ducking behind a tree. Robyn and Wren followed suit. There were five more men ahead, walking in the direction of the farm.

A radio suddenly squawked to life. "Hoggy and Johnstone are down. I want all teams back in the forest now. We're going to spit-roast these bitches."

The radio transmission had broadcast in front of them, but they could actually hear the words coming from the man talking into the radio just a few metres behind them as well. "Oh god," Georgie hissed.

"Screw it," Robyn replied, they're not taking me alive. That's not going to be my life."

Wren pulled the self-cocking levers of her two crossbows and loaded them. Robyn drew an arrow from her quiver and looked across towards her sister. A few weeks before, her biggest concern had been whether she'd have a date for Friday night; funny how life could change.

"Not going to be mine either, sis," Wren said, looking across at her. Robyn nocked the arrow, pulled back her bowstring, and in once fluid movement, emerged from around the tree, bringing the sight window up to eye level and firing before her target even had chance to focus on the blur of movement in front of him.

Wren leapt out into the small clearing, brought both crossbows up at the same time. Robyn's arrow smashed through the ribcage of her target and he let out an agonised scream. The other four men all shot horrified glances towards him as they fumbled to raise their rifles.

Wren fired and the two bolts whistled through the air; she crouched a little and gently allowed the bows to drop, slipping off the backpack straps from her shoulders before beginning to sprint towards the men. One of them creased over as the first bolt entered his abdomen, and another just stopped dead as it entered his forehead before he collapsed backwards, hitting the ground with a thud. The first shot boomed; the sound expanding through the forest and between the trees like a nuclear shockwave. Wren continued to run, expecting to fall any second, expecting to feel searing heat burrow into her gut, but it did not come. She heard another shot, this one from behind her, and the other man dropped to the ground, while there was an eruption of bark and woody flesh from the tree behind him.

Wren was now just a few feet away from the man who had fired the first shot. His rifle was pointing at her. Her eyes captured every micro-movement as if time was coming to a standstill. If he squeezed that trigger, it most surely would. She dived to the ground, twisting her body in mid-air and maintaining her forward momentum. As her head came back around, the soldier was adjusting his aim, trying to keep up with her lightning movement, all thoughts of leg shots now gone from his mind. His compatriots had fallen. This was a fight to the death. His eyes were murderer's eyes; Wren did not need more than a momentary glance to see that. She began to bounce back to her feet, her fingers searching out the handle of her knife from her belt. The barrel of the rifle loomed above her, slowly arcing down. She saw his finger beginning to move—she was too late.

20

Wren closed her eyes as the deafening blast-wave engulfed her. She kept them closed for a split-second eternity. Life and death shared that briefest time together. She felt something hot against her face; her eyes opened as a spurt of blood exploded from the shaft of the arrow that had shot through the soldier's neck. He fired the rifle again as he fell backwards with a look of pure shock on his face. The second shot was more muffled.

Wren's ears were ringing like the bells of St Paul's. There was shouting from behind her, but she had no idea what was being said. Suddenly, she caught movement from the corner of her eye. The man who had dived to the ground was scrambling back up, unaware that she had survived the shot, unaware that his pal was now heading down the infernal staircase to hell. He was taking aim towards Robyn.

Wren's banshee scream chilled the forest air as she brought her knife up, clutching it so hard that her knuckles turned white. She was on top of the other man in a heartbeat's echo. Her head and ears were still underwater, but her senses exploded to life once more as she felt the thick, hot, red blood glove her hand as she sunk the knife into the man's side over and over. Her left hand grabbed hold of his collar to support his already dying body. But death was not enough, not for the man who'd been about to take her sister's life. That was one step too far, and Wren descended into the primal, animalistic rage that slumbers in the heart of every human, despite centuries of civilisation.

When her explosive assault was over, Wren looked like Carrie at the prom. Tears streaked her face scoring pale streams through the blood. She and Robyn had come so far; they had fought so hard, and now it was going to end like this. The sound of another gunshot jolted her from her temporary madness and she looked up.

Robyn and Georgie were ducking around their respective trees, but on the other side now, more men emerged from the opposite direction. Wren stood and began to sprint towards them, placing the bloody knife back in her belt. Another shot went off and the forest floor erupted ahead of her. She scooped up her rucksack and crossbows and dove for cover. Wren crouched down, her back pressed tight against the bark of an oak. She looked across at her sister, who nocked another arrow, emerged from her cover for a moment, and fired. There was a brief pause then a howl of pain rose into the air.

Georgie leaned around from the tree she was using for cover, fired a single shot, and immediately ducked back as a hail of gunfire chipped the bark.

"What the hell are you doing?" shouted Baz to one of his men. "I told you, we need to take all of them back alive!"

"Screw that! They're slaughtering us and you want us to play nice? Game's over. TJ can go—" There was another boom, followed by a second of silence and then a muffled thud as a body fell to the ground.

"Anybody else want to disobey my orders?" Baz demanded.

More voices could be heard emerging from the north, then from the direction of the farm, and finally from the east. "We're surrounded," Georgie whispered with a pained look on her face.

Wren reloaded her crossbows and jumped out from behind her tree. She aimed both, fired and ducked back. Both bolts went astray as the remaining men either dropped to the floor or found cover. She immediately reloaded; this wasn't over.

"Listen to me, girls. You're surrounded. Lay down your weapons and come out. We won't hurt you," Baz's voice boomed.

Wren and Robyn looked towards each other from their respective trees. They both shook their heads slowly, then they looked towards Georgie. Tears had started running down her face as the realisation that she would never see Pippa again hit her.

"My pal's right," said another voice. All three women turned to see three men, fifteen metres behind them, out in the open, all with their guns aimed. "Now put down your weapons and—"

Georgie fired. Like a starter's pistol, it jolted Robyn and Wren into action. Wren fired both her crossbows and Robyn released her bowstring. The first man dropped, the bullet had hit him square in the chest; the second man staggered before falling. He brought his hand up to his neck as blood began to pour. He dropped his rifle, then, finally, he dropped to the ground as well. The final figure just stood there for a fraction of a moment, looking down at the bolt and the arrow sticking out of his stomach. His last breath left him. He fell backwards onto the forest floor; his head made a loud whoomph! as it smashed against a thick root emerging from the ground.

"Shit! They got Hawke," shouted one of the voices from behind them.

Wren reloaded her bows then placed them down and pulled the two Molotov cocktails from the side compartments of her rucksack. She grabbed the lighter from her pocket and lit them both as she heard the group of men led by the one they called 'Baz' running in her direction. She jumped out from behind her tree to see the gang clumped together just ten metres or so away. Wren flung the nail bomb as hard as she could, not at them, but at an angle towards a tree in front of them. At first, the men did not see what it was Wren had hurled, but as the bottle with the lit fuse shot towards the trunk, the realisation struck them and they dove to the ground.

The glass exploded against the tree, and with it, hundreds of flaming nails cartwheeled through the air. A moment later, the tree, its neighbour, the ground, and the men were all lit up in fiery torture. High pitched screams of pain rose up through the canopy. Burning metal plunged into flesh as a concoction of oil and diesel covered the men's clothing, their flesh, and their hair with liquid fire. They rolled around the floor, desperate to extinguish the flaming tendrils that licked against them, igniting the debris around them.

Wren, not really Wren anymore, but some wild creature fighting for her very survival, turned back around and picked up the other bottle just as the first figures from the north began to emerge. She hurled the second bomb in the same manner. Once again, it exploded in a lethal orange flare. Screams erupted and shouts of pain and rage wracked the air.

Wren picked up her rucksack and threw it over her shoulders. "Ruuunnn!!!" she yelled. The ringing in her ears was still there, but gradually dissipating as her feet, as well as her sister's and Georgie's, began to pound the compressed earth as they sprinted east.

Wren and Robyn leapfrogged over the three bodies that had fallen just a moment earlier, as Georgie came to a skidding halt. She bent down, pulling the radio from the belt of the man who had spoken to them, clipped it to her own and continued to run.

A few more seconds passed and the radio hissed to life. "This is Harmon," said a gruff voice. "Baz is down.

We're getting massacred out here. I'm assuming command. You see these bitches, you shoot to kill. No more messing about. Repeat, shoot to kill!"

Georgie turned the volume of the radio down and all three women immediately cast glances behind them, expecting to see a small army in pursuit. Instead, all they could see was a lot of smoke and a diminishing glow, as they weaved through the forest.

They continued, their eyes scouring the forest landscape, waiting for the next assault. Shouts echoed behind them, but gradually the sounds faded. The chatter on the radio became more desperate, and after several minutes of scouring the area, Harmon demanded they fall back to the farm and regroup.

Wren, Georgie and Robyn all stopped running as they approached the bank of a stream. They caught their breath, continually looking back in the direction they had come.

"I thought that was it. I thought we were goners there," Georgie said.

"We were. We should have been," Robyn said, looking towards her sister's blood-covered skin and clothes. "If it wasn't for your quick thinking, we wouldn't have made it."

Wren looked towards Robyn, her eyes wide, and suddenly tears welled up and began to fall as she replayed the last few minutes in her head. The frantic, uncontrollable stabbing frenzy; one explosion of flames, then another, as she had launched the Molotov cocktails. The burning bodies, the acrid smell of scorched flesh and clothing that had engulfed them as it rode on top of the burning oil and diesel.

Robyn went across to her sister; she knew why Wren was crying. It was no small thing to take a man's life. They had done it before and had nightmares before, but that...that had been hellish...a thing not just to give her nightmares, but of nightmares. "Come on," she said, taking

Wren's hand and walking her down to a rock by the stream. They both sat, still catching their breath, while Georgie brought the radio up to her ear, hoping to decipher any useful scrap of information. Robyn took a knife from her rucksack and cut a square out of her t-shirt. She dipped it in the cool stream, wrung it out, and began to wipe the blood from her sister's face.

"Erm, girls…we'd better keep going. They're heading back in on the quads."

"That's good," Robyn replied.

"What do you mean?"

"Have you heard the noise those things make? Yeah, they cover a lot of ground, but we'll hear them long before they see us."

"Good point."

"Just give me a minute," Robyn said, looking up at Georgie. Georgie looked towards Wren, then back at Robyn and nodded.

"You look so much like her," Wren said softly, her voice still quivering a little.

"Like who? Like Georgie?" she asked, worried that her sister was going a little doolally.

"No...like Mum. Remember when we'd get chocolate or jam or some crap over our mouths and chins and she used to wring out a face cloth, grab our heads and scrub it off like she was polishing brass or something?"

Robyn laughed. "Yeah, she wasn't what you'd call 'gentle,' was she?"

"You reminded me of her just then. When you were wiping my face. You've got a real look of her."

"We both have," Robyn replied, continuing to clean her sister's cheeks, but a little gentler now. "Are you okay, sis?"

"I will be."

"It was us or them. You realise that, don't you?"

"Yeah, I just...that's not it...I…"

"What is it then?" Robyn asked, pulling back a little.

"When I was stabbing that man...he was already dead and I just carried on; it was like I couldn't control myself."

"They were threatening us. Y'know, Wren, at the end of the day, humans are just animals. When you corner an animal and threaten its family, there's nothing it won't do to fight back. That's all you were doing. You were protecting your family from a predator, and the animal side took over," Robyn said smiling.

Wren looked at her for a moment. "Whoa! That is seriously deep for you."

"Yeah...I think I heard it on When Animals Attack once," she replied with a wide grin. She rinsed the cloth out again. "There. Come on, this day's got the potential to get a lot worse if we don't get a move on."

"Thanks, Bobbi."

"You'd do the same for me," she said, standing up and offering Wren her hand. Her sister grabbed it and climbed to her feet before the pair of them walked up the embankment to join Georgie.

"Okay. We must have covered at least half a mile, probably a bit more. I say we keep going east through the forest for a while, then sweep round in a big arc and head towards home. I just hope our plan works with the zombies."

"Trust me, it'll work," Robyn replied. "Every time there's a plume of smoke, those things head towards it like kittens to catnip, and trust me, you hang around with my sister for long enough and you get plenty of experience with this. Now, if I'm not much mistaken, a few minutes back, Wren set the forest on fire, so it might not be a bad idea for us to scarper before this place starts looking like Princes Street on a Saturday afternoon."

The three of them looked again in the direction they had come from, then turned and began to run.

21

Burwell climbed into the waiting Audi, and as soon as his door closed, it sped away. "Who the hell does Harmon think he is countermanding my orders," he asked as the car motored out of Aberfeldy towards the farm.

"I dunno…it sounded like we were getting ripped apart in there," said the driver.

"Seriously? You're telling me an army can't get three girls without it turning into a bloodbath?" He brought the radio up to his mouth and hit the talk button. "This is Burwell. Despite what Mr Harmon told you, I'm in command of this operation, and I'm telling you we're bringing those women in alive. I'm on my way to the farm now to get this shit-bomb cleaned up."

"We're not prepared to lose any more men to settle some grudge TJ has," came the response through the radio.

"Harmon? Harmon, is that you? The second we get back to Loch Uig, you're going to get the chance to say that to TJ's face. But right now, you'll stand down. You are not in charge here—I'm running things."

"Screw you!" came the response.

"Harmon? Harmon?" Burwell looked at the radio handset in disbelief. "He's turned it off. I can't believe that arse turned his radio off."

*

"Sounds like a mutiny," Georgie said.

"Let's hope," Wren said as the woodland began to lead up a hillside.

"Oh yeah, just what I need, a mountain climb. Can't we slow down a bit," Robyn said, coming to a stop and leaning against a tree.

"Bobbi, seriously, this is barely a mound, a tiny bump."

Robyn looked across at Wren then looked toward her sister's chest. "Well, I suppose you'd know."

For a second, Wren just looked, then she let out a small giggle. "Get lost. At least I never stuffed cotton wool under mine to make them look bigger than they are."

"I told you, they were chafing. I just used the cotton wool to stop the bra straps digging in."

"Yeah, right, a whole pack?"

"They were chafing a lot," Robyn said, smirking.

"Uh-huh." The three of them started to move once again, more slowly now as the gradient of the hill steepened.

They carried on for a few more minutes before arriving at a clearing. "Hang on a minute," Wren said, slipping her backpack off and placing her crossbows on the ground.

"What is it?" Georgie asked.

Wren pulled a pair of binoculars from her rucksack. "We've pretty much been running parallel with the farmland...I don't think we're that far in. If I can get high enough, I should be able to get a pretty good view of the surrounding area."

"Okay, but why?" Georgie asked.

"The fire in town has been burning a while now. Those things should be heading this way. When they do, coming after us will be the last thing those men will be thinking about," she said, placing the strap to the binoculars around her neck and starting to climb a tree.

"Be careful," Georgie said.

Wren stopped at a thick bough and swivelled her body around, bringing the field glasses up to her eyes. "What do you see?" Robyn asked.

For a while, Wren toggled the focus wheel, then panned the binoculars slowly up and left. She paused, then moved the focus wheel again before continuing. After a few seconds, she looked down towards Georgie and her sister.

"We're in real trouble."

*

The Audi's engine roared, echoing the bellowing rage that was growing inside Burwell as he headed towards the farm. "I swear, I'm going to—"

"Hold on!" screamed the driver, but it was too late.

Burwell was not wearing a seatbelt. He flew forward, smashing his head against the dashboard, letting out a pained scream as the Audi braked hard. Its tyres screeched on the surface of the road, and the driver did his best not to lose control of the vehicle as it skidded to a diagonal stop, ruffling the overgrown verge.

The driver looked across at Burwell, whose nose was bent to one side of his face. Blood poured over his mouth and down his chin. He scrambled from the footwell in a daze as the engine continued to idle.

"What the—" Burwell began to murmur, but stopped as he pushed his tongue forward to release two teeth from his mouth. He looked at the bloody roots in the palm of his hand then looked across towards the driver, whose attention was now fixed on the road ahead. Burwell felt lightheaded as the pain from his broken nose and shattered gums caught up with him. He slowly turned his head to see what the driver had nearly killed him for. Now, his pain was forgotten. "Moof...moof you idjut!" was the best he could manage to say as more blood began to gush from his mouth.

The driver slammed the gearstick into reverse. "Hold on," he said, and this time, Burwell stretched the seatbelt around his ample frame and clicked it into place.

He reached forward for the radio that he had dropped as the car had come to an abrupt halt. "This is Burwell. All teams head back to base, head back to Loch Uig," was what he tried to say, but it came out, "Thisus Brell. All tees heback to bus, heback to Luig!"

"Repeat!" demanded a voice as Burwell released the talk button.

The driver reversed the car into a passing place and did a quick three-point turn, making the tyres screech once more as he looked in the rear-view mirror. He grabbed the radio from Burwell. "All teams head back to base. Head back to Loch Uig now. There's an army of infected heading towards us. Get out now—repeat—get out." Gunfire began to sound and the driver looked towards Burwell, handing him the radio back. "That's the farm...they're done for." His eyes fixed on the rearview mirror again and he pressed his foot down to the floor.

*

When Wren had come up with the idea to divert the horde of creatures from Aberfeldy by starting a lorry fire, it had worked. The only problem was, it had worked too well. From the very moment Banks had stuffed his shirt into the diesel tank and lit it, the group had set something in motion. It would have caught up with them at some point, but fresh circumstances had prevailed and some point was now. The lorry had burned hot and bright. The blackest smoke had risen high into the blue sky, tickling the sun's own chin. The flames had spread to the hedgerows and bushes and the fire burned well into the night. The smoke could still be seen the following day, so Wren's plan had worked; the zombies of Aberfeldy were well and truly lured to the bait. As were the zombies of Aucterarder, Crieff, Dunkeld, Kenmore, Killin, Blairgowrie, and even the outskirts of Perth itself. That day, a low-lying cloud drowsed over the towns and villages to the north of Aberfeldy, otherwise, the horde massing around the vehicle would have been far greater. But what started as a few hundred ex-residents of the local village swelled to over six thousand.

The lorry burned away, and the mass of infected began to drift, slowly pouring into the surrounding countryside looking for fresh meat. But today—to be more precise, this very hour, this very minute—their voracious appetites had been piqued once again as every creature in range began to charge towards not one, but two, smoky black skyscrapers.

Fences and dry-stone walls collapsed as the charging masses thundered across fields like a giant hurricane of decay, spreading the gory paint of death over the green pastures and leaving behind meaty, foul-smelling chunks on torn barbed wire.

After days of fruitless searching, the game was on again. And as fields converged, so, too, did the creatures. Squads became platoons. Platoons became companies. Companies became battalions...all the time growing stronger, creating more devastation. Their excited growls began to rumble ever louder, making the very air vibrate with the demonic warning that Hell was coming.

*

"I don't feel very well," Robyn said, bringing the binoculars down from her eyes. She and Georgie had climbed into the tree as Wren struggled to put into words the full extent of the nightmare that was approaching.

"We need to get higher," Georgie said.

"What, you can't see how royally screwed we are from here? You want to get a better look?" Robyn asked.

"No, I mean, we need to get higher up the hill," Georgie replied.

"Why? What good will that do?"

"The fires are to the west of us. Even if those things are coming from the east, they're not going to struggle up a hill when there is so much flat land around. I know they're dumb, but they seem to be pretty single-minded when it comes to reaching their potential prey."

"Georgie's right," Wren said. "That's our best option. Actually, it's our only option."

The three of them scrambled back down the tree and, despite the mounting fatigue, they started their climb up the hill. Back on the forest floor and in between all the trees, they were well shielded from the fields of the undead that were marauding their way. When firing started out of the blue, for a moment they panicked, but the panic did not last long as they soon realised it was something that would help draw the creatures off in another direction.

*

Harmon stormed out of the farmhouse as he heard the shots. The radio had just broadcast a message telling all teams to fall back, and that was his intention—until he reached the farmyard and realised it was already too late. Multiple creatures emerged from around the house and farm buildings. Harmon's men were firing; they had dealt with the infected before.

Beast after beast fell to the ground as more and more emerged. "The bus!" Harmon yelled. "Get back to the bus!"

There were just eight men in the vicinity of the farmyard. The rest were in the woods, searching for the women, but not for much longer. Another volley of gunfire took down more of the creatures, then all the men rushed towards the coach, bounding up the steps. Harmon was the last in. He pushed the lever, closing the folding door with a whoosh. Immediately, a group of creatures threw themselves towards it, making it shudder.

The bus had been armoured, and a door-sized metallic plate was hinged, but Harmon had not had time to pull it to, so the pneumatic door was all that stood between the occupants of the coach and the beasts.

All the windows had been replaced by metal sidings with letterbox sized holes cut out for rifles to poke through.

Right now, though, the eight men had no intention of doing anything other than heading into the darkness of the bus and holing up in the hope that something else would divert attention away from them.

They crouched down in the aisle, giving the creatures no chance to see movement from within. "What do we do?" asked one of the men in no more than a whisper.

"Keep your mouth shut, Davis," Harmon hissed.

Multiple gunshots began to sound in the forest as more of the massive undead army invaded the trees.

"Why don't we try and drive out of here? The rest of them are done for anyway."

"Cos we don't have the keys, do we? Now keep schtum," Harmon responded.

"Why? Who's got the keys?"

"Baz took them to make sure nobody ran out."

"Why didn't we get them off him?"

Harmon grabbed Davis by the scruff of the neck. "Cos I only found out when I got back here, didn't I?"

"So we're trapped."

"I swear, if you don't shut your mouth, you're going to be a goner long before anyone else."

More beasts crowded around the bus and slowly it began to sway, like a rowboat on an increasingly choppy sea. The feverish growls and smell of rot seeped into the coach, coating everything in a film of festering putrescence.

"I can't take this...I can't take this," Davis said, his voice no longer a whisper as further panic set in.

There was a blurred movement, and it was all over. Harmon had thrust his knife blade up through Davis's throat. There was a sound, like air escaping a tyre, and that was it. Harmon hoisted his dead body onto one of the seats, wiped off his blade, and his hand and crouched down once more. Despite the growing noise, despite the increasing movement, nobody else said a word.

*

Robyn, Wren and Georgie finally reached the summit of the slope. Cover was provided by dense growth of pines, and unless a horde of rampaging creatures literally came face to face with them, the chances of being spotted by man or beast were negligible. The three of them stood there for a moment, catching their breath.

The shooting had stopped as quickly as it had started, and that could only mean one thing, but none of them were in the mood to celebrate, because it wasn't yet clear if the same fate awaited them.

The growls continued to drift towards them like a lament for lost souls, and the vibration of pounding feet made the air itself tremble in fear of what approached.

"What now?" Robyn asked.

"Now we wait," Wren replied.

"For how long?"

Wren looked towards Georgie, whose blank expression told her she had no more of an idea than Wren. "I don't know, sis...until it's safe for us to move."

"Oh good. For a second there I thought we didn't have a plan," Robyn replied.

"Look, Robyn, I don't want to have to spend a minute longer here than I need to. I want to get back to Pippa and Mum...and Dad. But we can hardly try to make an escape when the fields, the forests, the roads are full of those things, can we? We're just going to have to be patient."

Wren slipped her rucksack off, arched her back and stretched her arms. "I think we might very well have to spend the night up here at least."

"Oh great. At least we can provide dinner for the midges," Robyn replied, batting away a small cloud of the insects, "before we provide breakfast for the zombies."

Wren rolled her eyes and walked to the edge of the plateau. Despite the thick foliage, she was able to see down to the fields. Wave after wave of creatures ploughed across them. It was never-ending. It was as if the gates of hell had opened up and every demon since the dawn of time itself was marching their way.

22

The coach rocked more with each passing moment. Stifled gasps fluttered in the darkness as the men took tighter grips on the grab rails to steady themselves.

"This is no good, mate. We're not going to make it," whispered one of the men.

"Well, what do you want me to do? I can't just magic a set of keys, Taylor," Harmon replied.

"Can't we try and hotwire it or something?"

"Too modern. We wouldn't be able to get around the immobiliser. It's not like the old days," Harmon replied.

"Okay, well what about—" there was a sudden thud followed by a metallic screech, unlike any sound that they'd heard before. Now the excited growls became even louder as the door shifted in its track.

"That's it. We're done!" Harmon cried as more light than before bled into the bus. "The door's about to go."

All the men climbed to their feet and raised their rifles except Harmon. Another bang shook the bus, and the pneumatic door folded a little more. "What do we do? What do we do?" Taylor repeated frantically.

Harmon finally stood up and walked to the back of the bus, slumping down on the seat. He placed his rifle down beside him as the door edged open even further. He retrieved a packet of cigarettes from his shirt pocket, flicking one out and placing it between his lips. He pulled out his lighter and sucked deeply as the flame met the end of the tobacco rod. Suddenly, everything went silent other than that sound he loved so much, that sweet crackling as those magical dry leaves began to burn. He inhaled deeply, and even in the subdued light of the coach interior, he could see the mesmerising blue cloud dance up in front of him.

A smile came to his lips only to vanish again just as quickly. Suddenly, all his senses woke once more in a blinding, deafening eruption. The door caved in and before the terrified guards could identify a target, they began firing indiscriminately. Light poured through the doorway followed by a shrouding darkness as the mass of creatures stormed the bus. The odd one fell as a lucky shot brought it down, but futility gave way to resignation as the guards realised they were merely prolonging their suffering.

One by one they fell as teeth and claw-like fingers tore their flesh. Not just growls but now screams as well filled the bus. Pushing past the familiar burn of smoke, the smell of decay and that of fresh, coppery blood invaded Harmon's nasal passages as he desperately tried to enjoy his last cigarette. The last guard fell in a panicking, screaming fit of agony in front of him, and that's when Harmon knew his time had come. The creatures surged towards him; he took a final, long puff. He began to exhale, but before he could, darkness surrounded him.

There was nothing pleasant, nostalgic or satisfying in his final memory. It was one of suffering, pain and sadness. It cloaked him in a frigid shadow, and as his eyes blinked shut, the cold and the darkness reached new depths. Harmon's heart began to stutter, but before it gave in for good, a tear appeared in the corner of his eye. He'd not been a good man. He had done many wicked things in his life. He had once stood up in a court of law to have sentence passed upon him, and the judge had called him evil. But now he knew, as a second tear joined the first, that the judge knew nothing. For the judge, evil had merely been a lazy description for a flawed, immoral criminal. Now, for the first time in his life, Harmon really knew what evil was. It began to consume him, one cell at a time, like some flesh-eating virus. In the final seconds of his life, Harmon had an epiphany. Hell was not a place; it was a state of being.

*

Wren looked in the direction of the shots she'd heard mere seconds before, and now she wished she hadn't. Yes, there was plenty of smoke to attract the creatures, but now there were flames, too. She estimated that when she had launched the Molotov cocktails, she had been fifty or sixty metres away from the tree-line. Now, though, she looked across to see flames licking and scorching the tree-line itself. Orange whips lashed up, racing the dancing black swirls to the top.

The fire spat and jumped, and suddenly another tree had caught. The summer had been uncharacteristically warm, and the forest had now become one giant tinderbox.

Wren angled her head down to look at Robyn and Georgie who had planted themselves at the base of a tree. They were sharing a bottle of water and staring blankly ahead, still in shock.

"We've got to go," Wren said.

"We discussed this, Wren. We're going to have to wait a while," Georgie replied.

"No. You don't understand."

Georgie looked up towards Wren, who was looking towards the farmhouse once again. "What? Why?"

"It's easier if you come have a look," Wren replied.

Georgie and Robyn gave each other a concerned glance and climbed to their feet. They walked slowly towards the tree Wren was perched in. There was a big part of them that didn't want to see what she had seen. They had been through enough for one day, for one lifetime, and now, apparently, there was more trouble on their heels.

They wearily scaled the trunk, carefully placing their feet and grabbing the strongest looking branches until they took their places at either side of Wren and just stared.

"That's erm...that's not good," Robyn said.

"Jesus. That will be here in no time," Georgie said, turning to look south, "and so will they." Her eyes lingered on the army of zombies still charging over the fields.

"Yeah," added Robyn, "and the more the flames and smoke spreads, the more those things will spread out too."

"We need to continue heading east," Wren said.

"That just takes us further and further from home," Georgie replied.

"Right now we don't have a choice. We head east as fast and as far as we can to escape the fire, to escape these things. At some point, there'll be somewhere we can rest, but this isn't it," Wren said.

Wren climbed back down, jumping the last few feet. Robyn followed her and slowly walked back across to collect her bow and rucksack. Georgie remained in the tree a while longer, her heart sinking further. Eventually, she broke her gaze and started to climb down. There was a sudden crack as a bough snapped beneath her feet.

"Aaarrgh!" she screamed. Pine needles and branches caned her as she dropped to the ground. Wren and Robyn looked across at the moment of impact to see her ankle buckle underneath her as she fell.

"Oh no," Wren muttered.

"Arrrggghhhh!" Georgie screamed, even louder this time.

Both sisters ran across to her. Her face was cut and grazed, and now her teeth gritted in an attempt to stifle further grunts of pain.

"Georgie!" Wren gasped as she knelt down beside her. Robyn crouched down at the other side.

"Just give…me a minute," Georgie said.

Robyn and Wren sat for a moment. "I've got some painkillers and bandages in my rucksack," Wren finally said.

A confused look swept over Georgie's face. "You carry bandages and painkillers around?"

"Ha! I told you that wasn't normal," Robyn said.

"No, but…it's smart," Georgie said, slowly leaning up onto her elbows. She set her jaw as she looked down towards her foot. It wasn't shooting off at a weird angle as she'd expected, but it still hurt like mad. Robyn and Wren took an arm each and slowly sat her up

"You want me to untie your boot?" Wren asked.

"Would you?" Georgie grimaced, despite Wren unfastening the laces and pulling the boot and sock off her friend's foot as gently as she could. All their eyes widened to see how red and swollen the joint had become in the space of a minute.

"Can you move it?" Wren asked.

Georgie winced as she slowly rotated her foot. "I could really use those painkillers," she said.

Wren nodded and immediately went to retrieve the self-assembled first aid kit from her bag. "I think it's a sprain," Wren said. "I've had quite a few. Shame we haven't got any ice."

Georgie continued to move her foot around. "I think you're right, but I'm going to struggle to walk."

"We can help you," Robyn replied.

"First things first. I need to get this strapped up," Wren said, handing Georgie the box of painkillers.

Georgie flipped out three, placed them in her mouth and took a drink from the bottle of water while Wren got to work strapping her ankle. She closed her eyes, fighting the pain, and at the same time weighing the options ahead of her.

Wren wrapped the final layer of bandage around and slid in the safety pin, careful not to prick Georgie's skin. "That feels a little better already," she said.

Wren carefully slid the sock back on and then the boot, tying the laces tightly to add as much ankle support as she could. "Bobbi, can you find a branch or something big enough to use as a crutch or a stick?"

"Course," Robyn replied, standing and disappearing into the trees.

"Thank you, Wren," Georgie said.

"Don't thank me yet, we need to get you standing first."

Robyn returned a moment later with a thick branch that came up to her shoulder. "Aarrgghh, mateys," she said, doing her best Long John Silver impersonation and using the bough to take her body weight while she pranced around on one leg.

The others let out a small laugh. "You missed your vocation in life, you should have been—"

"A pirate?" Robyn said continuing to hop around.

"Well, I was going to say on the stage," Georgie replied.

"What, sweeping it?" Wren asked.

"Ha Ha, very funny. My drama teacher said I was a natural."

"A natural drama queen more like."

Robyn placed the crutch on the ground and knelt back down. Georgie placed her arms around Robyn and Wren's shoulders and the two girls slowly took their friend's weight as they rose to their feet. Georgie kept her ankle raised as she stood, putting as much weight as she could on her left foot. She balanced on it until Robyn handed her the crutch. She carefully positioned it underneath her right armpit before putting her weight on it fully and attempting to move. She grimaced as the branch dug into her, but slowly walked a small circuit before resting against a tree.

"Thank you," Georgie said, looking at both girls. "You two are amazing. Two of the most amazing people I've ever met. To have come through this thing the way you have…I'm pretty certain you can do anything."

"I don't think—"

"You need to leave me," Georgie said, interrupting Wren.

"What?" Robyn and Wren asked at the same time.

"If I go with you, we're all going to die the second we run into those things. I need you to go. I need you to get back to the Manor and tell them all to get the hell out of there. They need to run and keep running until they're well clear of this whole place. Those men from Loch Uig will spread out like a virus until they've infected and invaded this whole area. I need you to tell my mum and dad to take Pippa and get to safety, wherever that is. You've got to—"

"Screw that," Robyn said. "No way. We're not leaving you."

"Don't be stupid. I can barely hobble. We won't even be able to escape the forest before the flames reach us, never mind what happens when we run into those things."

"We're not leaving you," Wren said just as adamantly as her sister.

"I'm not giving you a choice," Georgie said pulling the Glock 17 from her belt and placing the muzzle of it against her temple.

Wren put her hands up placatingly. "Georgie don't be stupid—don't do this."

"Then do as I ask," she replied as tears began to run down her face.

"Georgie—"

"Pippa is everything. She is the single greatest thing I've done with my life. I need to know she's safe. I believe in you girls. You can do this. You can get back there and warn them."

"Yeah, and how do you rate our chances if you pull that trigger and tell every zombie in those fields, every one at that farm, every one running through the forest that we're up here? How do you rate our chances then?" Robyn demanded.

Georgie paused and brought the gun away from her head suddenly looking at it in a new light. "I—"

"Listen, how's this for a deal? I promise you, we'll get back to the Manor. We'll tell them, but you put that gun down. We all head out of here together. If we run into a situation, then we'll go, just Bobbi and me, we'll go, we'll keep our promise, and you can use that gun. You can use it to give us more time, to make sure they don't get you, hell, take a few of them out, whatever you want. But don't use it now…please," Wren said.

Georgie looked at Wren, then towards Robyn. "You give me your word, both of you."

"I give you my word," Wren said.

"Robyn?"

Robyn let out a long breath. "You want me to tell you I'll abandon you and let you kill yourself if we run into trouble? What kind of person does that make me?"

"One who will give my daughter a chance to live. Because right now she has none. If we don't get back there, if we don't warn them, those men will head there and then it's all over. Then your good intentions will have killed my daughter or imprisoned her to a hell I don't want to even imagine. So do you give me your word?"

Robyn looked long and hard at Georgie then lowered her head towards the ground. When she spoke they could barely hear her.

"Yes."

179

23

Burwell felt like a man faced with a firing squad as he sat down in front of Fry and TJ. "Look, I know what you're going to say," he began.

"No...no you don't. You have no idea," Fry said

"Look, if you'd have given me free rein, I could have put this to bed quickly, but no, TJ wanted those girls back here so we had to go in with kid gloves, we had to make—"

TJ was about to say something when Fry beat him to it. "So let me get this straight; this was TJ's fault," he said, standing up slowly.

"I'm not saying that, all I'm saying is—"

"It sounds like what you're saying to me. In fact, it sounds exactly like that to me," Fry said, placing his hands behind his back and beginning to stroll around the long meeting room table. "'You could have put it to bed quickly, but TJ asked for those girls to be brought back.' Isn't that what you said?"

"Well, yeah, but—"

"TJ is like my right hand. He's been with me as long as I can remember. If an order comes from him, it comes from me. So are you saying it was my fault?" Fry asked, stopping in mid-step and turning towards Burwell.

Burwell's cheeks turned cherry red and he felt his palms begin to sweat as Fry burned holes through him with his blazing blue eyes. "I misspoke. What I meant was—"

"You misspoke? And what did you do in Aberfeldy? You missed the pot. You did a great big stinking dump, and you left it steaming over the sides of the pot," Fry said starting to walk again. In the space of a sentence, Fry's face had turned red as his rage began to boil. "You lose men, vehicles…you lose weapons and ammunition. Now maybe…just maybe I could get my head around that if you'd brought back something more valuable." He walked around the far end of the table to the side Burwell was sat on and slowly began to advance towards him, flicking every chair with his middle finger on the way back down. "But no, you brought back nothing."

"I told you, we split up and checked out a couple of places before regrouping in Aberfeldy. We got a shout from our advance team that a convoy was heading our way and we set a trap. We—"

"And these places you checked out…what did you get from them?" Fry asked, stopping directly behind Burwell's chair.

"Well, nothing. Turns out they'd already been turned over," Burwell replied.

"And what were these places? What was worth deviating from the original plan for?"

"One was an office block just on the other side of town that one of the lads had seen on a previous visit; the other was a discount store," Burwell replied.

"Brilliant. Just what you need when you're in the middle of Armageddon, a good supply of office stationery and a load of cheap plastic shite made in some Chinese sweatshop that'll fall apart the second you get it out of the packet."

"We just thought there might have been—"

"No. You didn't think. You didn't think at all. You shit the bed and then tried to blame everyone else."

"No, it's not like that. I—"

Fry grabbed Burwell's thick, black, greasy hair in his left fist, clamped his chin in his right hand, and twisted with juggernaut force. There was a loud crack, and Burwell flopped forward onto the table.

"How's your arm?" Fry asked.

"Like new," TJ responded.

"I should have sent you down there."

"Yeah, you should."

Fry's eyes narrowed slightly, then his face broke into a smile. "Can you sort this mess? Make sure there are no more mistakes?"

"You know I can. We'll go the long way around, avoid the whole area."

Fry looked at TJ long and hard. "Do it."

*

"Stop—this is madness," Georgie said. "We're not getting anywhere. The fire's getting closer all the time, it'll be on us before we know it."

"I don't think so," Wren replied, pulling a bottle from her backpack and taking a drink before handing it to Georgie.

"Oh yeah, how do you reckon?"

"The wind's changed direction slightly. It was coming right up behind us before, but it's shifted a little. That should give us more time."

Georgie took a drink and passed the bottle on to Robyn. "Actually, I hadn't noticed."

"Yeah, you find most normal people don't get half the stuff Wren notices," Robyn said, taking a drink.

"Do you need to rest longer?" Wren asked.

"Just a little," Georgie replied, lifting her arm to reveal a bloody armpit.

"Oh god," Wren said. "That must be agony!"

"It's not the nicest feeling in the world."

Wren took off her jacket and sliced through the seam of one shoulder and then the other, turning it into a gilet. "Here we go, problem solved. This'll give you some padding," she said, putting her new creation on. She looked down at her bare arms and smiled. "I think this suits my badass image more," she said smiling.

"You're such a sweet girl, Wren," Georgie said, folding the material and placing it over the end of the branch for cushioning. "That's much better."

"You ready to carry on?" Wren asked.

"Yeah," Georgie nodded.

The trio began to walk again, the crackle of the fire behind them could still be heard occasionally, but now the intensity of the growls and the pounding feet had diminished to just the odd flurry.

"We'll carry on until we're out of the forest, find somewhere safe, and then grab a bite to eat," Wren said.

"Thank god. I'm starving," Robyn replied.

"You're always starving."

"Not my fault, I'm a growing girl."

"Yeah, I see your arse and thighs growing more every day," Wren said, smiling.

"You cheeky little—"

"Girls! Be nice to each other," Georgie said. Robyn and Wren both laughed. "What's so funny?"

"That's exactly what Mum used to say," Robyn replied. "You've even got her tone of voice."

"Way to make me feel old, thanks."

"I didn't mean it like that," Robyn said.

"I know, I was only—" The smile disappeared from Georgie's face in an instant and she stopped walking. Robyn and Wren stopped too, looking at her, wondering what was wrong. "Oh my god!" she whispered, continuing to stare straight ahead through the trees.

Robyn turned first and immediately saw what had stopped Georgie in her tracks. Without pause, she drew an arrow and raised the sight up to her eye.

Wren dropped to the ground, sliding the rucksack from her back at the same time. The group of creatures had not seen them yet, but it was only a matter of time. Then it happened; one of them caught a glimpse of the three women, and suddenly all fourteen were hurtling through the trees towards them.

"Far left," Robyn shouted, releasing the string.

"Far right," Wren shouted before she had even finished placing the second arrow into the crossbows. She lined both of them up and fired, immediately pulling the first, then the second self-cocking lever before placing two more bolts into position. When she looked back up, both of her first targets were on the ground, and Robyn's second arrow was gliding towards another beast.

Georgie used the nearest tree to prop herself up and took aim. "No!" Robyn shouted, nocking a third arrow. "If there are more in the area we'll have them all on top of us." She fired, and another beast flew backwards as if the ground had been whipped from beneath its feet.

Wren fired two more bolts. One sunk straight into one of the beast's eyes, the second deflected off the side of another's temple and disappeared. "Damn," Wren said, immediately reloading. "They're coming too fast."

Robyn fired another arrow; a split second later, a seventh creature went down. She drew yet another, then another, but Wren was right—they were coming too fast. Two more bolts fired from Wren's bows.

Wren dropped the bows and ran across to Georgie, grabbing her crutch and starting to sprint straight towards the four remaining beasts. Even after all this time, as familiar as the sights and sounds of these abominations had become, they still sent chills down Wren's spine. The four creatures all converged on her. She took another lightning stride and now, there were just a few feet between her and the beasts' demonic clutches. There was a sudden blur, and the second creature in line collapsed as one of Robyn's arrows burrowed through its forehead.

Other than diverting attention and giving Robyn more time, Wren hadn't really thought about what she was going to do, but now she saw an opportunity. She brought the crutch up, clenching it in both fists in front of her chest, then she dove towards the gap her sister had created. Her knuckles hit the ground as she began her forward roll, her movement so lithe, so swift, the creatures' clumsy attempts to grab her merely sent them more off-balance as the crutch knocked their very feet from beneath them.

The three beasts toppled forward, the force of their momentum dragging the sturdy branch from Wren's clutches. She finished her forward roll, springing back to her feet and swivelling back around to face them. The creatures began to clamber; an arrow disappeared through the top of one's head, and then there were two. Wren pulled the knife from her belt, her heart was racing, her throat was dry, her palms were sweating as the first, then the second, monster rose. When they did not turn towards her, she felt a momentary relief, but her heart quickly sank. Like lions trapping the slowest antelope, the two beasts began to tear towards Georgie.

Georgie remained propped against the tree, her Glock still in her hand. Using it might save her for a short time, but would bring huge danger to the girls. Not using it would mean her own death, but give Robyn and Wren the time they needed to put these things down. "Remember our deal," she shouted, dropping her gun to the ground. She let happy memories invade her thoughts. The first time she held Pippa in her arms; Pippa's first steps; Pippa's first words; Pippa, Pippa, Pippa. Tears welled in her eyes as two infernal creations charged towards her. Their outstretched fingers swam through the warm forest air, opening and closing like lobster pincers. Their guttural growls gurgled in the back of their throats, and their pupils danced in fevered anticipation as they sped towards fresh meat.

Georgie closed her eyes and waited. She felt the gentle tickle of her salty teardrops as they ran down her cheeks over her lips. The last thing she had witnessed was a scene of horror, a scene from hell, but now her favourite photo of PIppa emerged from the dark in her mind's eye. Pippa...her one true success. Pippa—

"Aaarggghhh!!!"

24

Georgie's eyes shot open as the animalistic scream dragged her from a happier place and time. It took her a moment to focus. One of the creatures was collapsing backwards with the shaft of an arrow protruding from the bridge of its nose.

Wren was leaping through the air, having grabbed the other beast by the scruff of its neck. Its fingers were less than a foot away from Georgie's face as Wren plunged her knife blade through the roof of its head. Its eyes flicked shut and the ghoulish sounds immediately halted as the creature crumpled forward, colliding with Georgie. Wren's scream turned from that of a barbaric battle cry to one of surprise, and now Georgie joined in too as all three of them crashed to the ground. There was no movement for a few seconds, then Wren rolled away from the pile-up onto her back, desperate to bring her breathing under control.

Robyn threw a final glance in the direction the creatures had approached from to make sure the coast was clear, then she walked across and hauled the slain monstrosity from Georgie, who lay there with a look of disgust and horror on her face like she had just been run over by a plague of sewer rats. The beast slumped to one side and Georgie turned her head to look at it in all its gruesomeness.

"I thought I was going to die...I'd...I'd said goodbye," she said in a daze.

"Yeah well, maybe next time, if you're lucky," Robyn replied extending her hand.

Georgie reached out and grabbed it, putting all her weight on her left foot as Robyn hoisted her to her feet. She leaned back against the tree to catch her breath.

"That was close," Wren said, climbing to her feet.

"How did you do it? How did you girls survive out here so long?" Georgie asked.

"Just like this," Wren replied. "We fought. Those are the only two options, fighting or dying." She walked across to collect the crutch and grabbed the jacket sleeves from the ground, folding them back over and placing them on top of the jagged branch edge. "Here you go." She handed it to Georgie.

"Thank you," Georgie replied, laughing in relief.

"Come on, we'd better keep going. The sooner we can find somewhere safe, the better," Wren said.

The group gathered their belongings and continued their trek, now with even more trepidation than before. At one point, a rustling bush made Robyn draw an arrow ready to fire, but it turned out to be two squirrels abandoning their hidey-hole as the humans approached.

The woodland thinned out and gave way to a scraggy field. They surveyed it for several minutes before finally breaking cover. The grass was tall and would provide good camouflage if they needed to duck down quickly. They were a hundred metres or so clear of the forest when they looked back to see the vast columns of smoke reaching towards the sky.

"Oh my god!" Wren said.

"So, that's a row of shops, a monastery, a hotel, and now an entire forest. Nice going, sis," Robyn said, "really good work."

"I didn't do the monastery, and technically, the hotel was an accident," Wren said looking towards the blaze guiltily.

"Uh-huh," Robyn replied. "Come on. We need to keep...oh shit!!!"

Wren and Georgie immediately turned. The path directly ahead was clear, but now, bobbing heads could be seen occasionally popping up from the grass to the north and south like shark fins in water. Robyn, Wren and Georgie were on a plateau, albeit an uneven one. Emerging at diagonals to the left and to the right were dozens of beasts.

"Oh no," Wren said.

"What do we do?" Robyn asked.

"We can't go back into the forest. We can't go left, we can't go right. We go straight ahead or we stay put," Wren replied.

"They're going to converge on us whatever we do. It's just a matter of time," Georgie said.

Wren looked ahead then looked towards the two approaching hordes. "No...no, I don't think so. C'mon we need to be quick." She started running.

"Wren... Wren?" Robyn said, placing the bow between her back and the rucksack and taking the crutch from Georgie. Georgie placed her right arm around Robyn's shoulder, Robyn placed her left arm around Georgie, and the two of them began to move as fast as they could.

Wren flew through the tall grass as the figures to either side of her grew slightly bigger. She came to a shuddering stop as the grass gave way to...nothing. Wren put her arms out, ready to fly, but thankfully, it didn't come to that as she managed to regain her balance. Directly their front, a long-forgotten quarry had been chiselled out of the landscape. Thirty metres below was a lake of bottle-green water shimmering in the sun. Jagged rocks stuck out from the cliff face, and beneath the surface of that water could be anything, but on the other side of the wide canyon was a way out.

Wren looked left and right as the creatures began to draw level. Soon they would be heading towards her—two foul-smelling speed trains with gnashing teeth on a collision course with her in the middle. She looked behind her. "Careful!" she shouted as Robyn and Georgie approached.

"Oh crap!" Robyn said. "We're totally stuffed." She gave the crutch back to Georgie, pulled her bow free, and drew an arrow from one of her quivers as the first creatures began to head around the mouth of the quarry towards them.

"No," Wren stopped her. "This is our way out."

"What?" Robyn and Georgie screeched simultaneously.

"We can make it," Wren said, looking down.

"Wren, that water could be two feet deep for all we know. And even if it isn't, if it's fifty feet deep, at this height it's a really risky jump. That's not even to mention those rocks sticking out all the way down," Georgie said, looking over the edge.

"We're out of options," Wren said, looking in both directions towards the ever-increasing mass of creatures.

"I hate to say this, but she's right," Robyn said.

The three of them all stood there, staring down at the calm water as the drumming feet pounded ever nearer. "Oh god," Georgie said.

"Honest this'll work," Wren said. "It's just like in Butch Cas—"

"I swear if you finish that sentence, I'm going to shoot you with one of my arrows," Robyn said.

"I'll go first," Wren said. She was about to jump, then quickly rushed towards her sister and threw her arms around her. "Love you, Bobbi."

"Yeah. Love you too."

Wren hugged Georgie, too. "Don't worry. We'll get back to the Manor," she said before turning around, taking one long stride, and leaping high and wide into the air.

Robyn and Georgie watched her as she flew, until suddenly, she was not flying anymore, she was plummeting. She put her arms out and made circular motions with her hands. Her body remained stiff and upright. One second she was there, and the next, she was gone, replaced by a temporary geyser as water shot up into the air. Robyn clutched Georgie's arm tightly, she held her breath, her stomach turned over and she felt sicker with each moment that Wren did not reappear at the surface. Then, a head broke through the rippling water, followed by shoulders and arms. "Don't jump with your rucksack on. It nearly took my arms off when I landed," Wren shouted up.

Robyn immediately unhitched her rucksack, her bow, her quivers; she threw each one down in the hope that Wren would be able to get them before they disappeared beneath the murky surface, but that was only a small consideration now as she looked first left, then right. A few more seconds and the creatures would be upon them. Robyn took hold of Georgie's hand, as her friend dropped her crutch into the quarry.

"One...two...three," Robyn said, and they both leapt. For a second they remained silent as the air rushed beneath them and the rippling green water loomed ever closer, but then, like children on a fairground ride, they both let out frightened screams until SPLOOSH! The water exploded around them.

Wren's head bobbed under as the waves sloshed over her. The rucksack was only half full, but it still weighed a tonne wet. She continued to tread water, tiring quickly, but that was the least of her concerns as she waited for Robyn and Georgie to reappear. Wren had managed to grab Robyn's bow and the quivers, but her rucksack was gone...down to the bottom of the quarry, however deep that was.

The water parted and Robyn's head appeared. She sucked in lungfuls of fresh air before swimming over to Wren. They both looked up to see the creatures beginning to gather around the edge of the cliff, but there was still no sign of Georgie. A few more seconds passed, and then they saw her, although they wished they hadn't. Her body floated up, face down, and Robyn swam across, flipping her over in the water. Her eyes were closed and her head lolled to one side.

"We need to get to the shore quick," Wren said.

Both of them started to swim, but it was slow going. Wren was weighed down by the rucksack, along with the bow and quivers, while Robyn struggled with Georgie's limp body.

"Oh god no!" Robyn said, looking back up towards the cliff as two creatures were inadvertently barged off the top by the growing throng. The first fell headfirst, smashing its skull against a jutting rock before splashing down at the base of the cliff. The second cartwheeled through the air before a chilling thud echoed around the quarry as it landed heavily on a ledge.

Robyn turned back to her direction of travel and swam as fast as she could. She had her lifesaver medal from swimming at school, but that had just been with a plastic dummy. Georgie was a lot heavier, and as much as the adrenalin was pumping through Robyn, her arms and legs were beginning to ache.

Wren was surging ahead towards the shore. She heard a loud splash and turned to see water jetting up from the base of the cliff. Another of the creatures must have fallen in; she could only hope it was dead on impact. She had enough to worry about without the thought of hands grabbing at her feet from beneath the surface, or worse still, grabbing at her sister while she was struggling with Georgie. She turned back and started kicking harder. Her arm strokes were limited as she held onto the bow and quivers, but eventually, the water became more shallow and she felt her feet hit against the bottom. She slowly climbed out as her dripping wet clothes clung to her. Wren dropped the bow and quivers, pulled the rucksack from her back and turned, wading back into the lake as three more creatures plummeted from the clifftop at the far end of the quarry.

Robyn was still about twenty metres in and clearly struggling. Another fountain of water spewed upwards as a further creature disappeared beneath the surface. A shiver ran down Wren's spine as she realised there was something worse than seeing these creatures...not seeing them. She trudged back in up to her waist then dived, kicking her legs as fast as she could as she now swam unencumbered.

"Are...they...behind us?" was all Robyn could say as her head bobbed up and down in the water.

Wren reached her sister. "Can't see anything. I'll take over, Bobbi. You just concentrate on getting to the shore," she said, placing her arm around Georgie and doing her best to keep her head above the surface as she continued to swim. She heard more loud splashes behind her and watched as her sister swam to land, finally dragging herself to her feet. The water poured from her as she plodded the last few metres to the shore. More loud splashes sounded and Wren's heart raced even faster.

"Come on, sis!" Robyn shouted.

Wren's mind began to work overtime as she heard more of these creatures plunging into the lake. Can these things swim? Or will they sink to the bottom and walk across the quarry bed? Would she feel a hand seize her ankle and drag her down? Panic seized her as her foot touched something in the water. It was momentary, but her body froze. Wren's arm tightened around Georgie. If she was going to die then at least she would not be alone, she would be with a friend. Her other foot hit something too, and that's when she realised they were close enough to the shore for her to wade the rest of the way in.

Robyn rushed out to meet them, keeping a careful eye on the water, making sure nothing emerged from the depths. She grabbed hold of one arm; Wren took Georgie's other, and they both dragged her to shore. They lay Georgie down on her back. "Oh god," Wren said, looking at her.

"Keep an eye on the water. I've got this...I can do this," Robyn said, kneeling down beside Georgie.

"Do what?"

"I did CPR on that course. I can do this..." Robyn said again.

Wren ran over to her rucksack, grabbed her two pistol crossbows, loaded them, and took guard at Robyn's side. She watched the water for any movement as another creature fell headlong from the top of the cliff like a lemming.

"God there are hundreds of them up there," Wren said.

Robyn ignored her comments and concentrated, thinking back to her course. "Georgie? Georgie?" she said, giving her a small shake. There was no response. She tilted Georgie's head back a little and opened her mouth checking to make sure it was clear. She put her ear close to Georgie's lips and looked at Georgie's chest, hoping to see movement, hoping to feel air against her face, but she felt and saw nothing. "Okay..." Pulling back, Robyn took a deep breath, and placed her left hand flat on Georgie's chest, putting her right on top of it. Then she began to pump. "One, two, three, four—"

Wren took her eyes away from the lake momentarily. "How many do you have to do?" she asked.

"I'm counting, Wren!" Robyn snapped back.

"Sorry." Wren shrank away a little and focussed her attention on the water once again.

"—seven, eight, nine..." she continued to thirty, and when there was still no response, she opened Georgie's mouth and pinched her nose before putting her own mouth over Georgie's lips and blowing two deep breaths. Out of the corner of her eye, she could see Georgie's chest rise, but that was all; she was still unresponsive.

She placed her hands, one over the other, back on Georgie's chest and began again. "Is she dead?" Wren asked weakly.

Robyn shot a glance towards her sister, but did not reply, she just carried on counting. "Fourteen, fifteen, sixteen…"

"Oh crap!" Wren said as a head suddenly bobbed out of the water. She brought one of her pistol crossbows up, aimed and fired. The trigger, the whole thing was wet to the touch, but as the bolt whistled towards its target, she let out a breath of relief…it still worked. The creature fell face down and disappeared back under the surface.

"Twenty-nine, thirty," Robyn said, immediately placing her mouth back over Georgie's and breathing gently two more times. She saw Georgie's chest expand again, but there was still no sign of her coming around.

"Is she dead, Bobbi?" Wren asked again.

"One, two, three, four…"

Two more heads popped out of the water. The moment the creatures set eyes on Wren, they had renewed purpose. Running was impossible. They fought against their liquid shackles and dragged their arms free. As they opened their mouths to sing a familiar song, sludge fell down their fronts, but now, their throats were clear once again and their hellish serenade began.

Wren dropped to the ground, picking up the already loaded bow, aiming and firing. The creatures continued to struggle; they were not the fast-moving devil's spawn they were on land. The bolt cracked through the cheekbone of the beast to the left and it splashed down into the water. Wren pulled back the self-cocking lever on the first bow, placing a bolt in before doing the same with the other. She could do this blindfolded now and as she loaded the second weapon, another head popped from the water, while three more creatures plunged from the clifftop above.

Another, then another head bobbed up. There were four coming straight towards them now; slowly, but deliberately, and she knew as sure as anything that more would follow. "Bobbi, we're in trouble here," she said, firing another bolt and then a second. One of the beasts fell face down, causing a second to stumble, while the other bolt sliced straight through the ear of its target. There was a minor, gory explosion, and the shot did nothing to alter the creature's course.

"Twenty-five, twenty-six, twen—"

Suddenly, Georgie spluttered. Water streamed from her mouth, and Robyn immediately turned her onto her side. The patient continued to cough as more water dribbled, then when her throat was finally clear she sucked in two lungfuls of air. Robyn put a reassuring hand on her upper arm.

"You did it!" Wren said excitedly, while kneeling back down to reload the crossbows.

Robyn gave herself just a few seconds. She took a breath then jumped to her feet, grabbing her bow and throwing the quivers onto her shoulder. She pulled an arrow and nocked it. She saw more creatures falling from the cliff. One plummeted head first to a jutting crag. It was like a melon exploding. It decorated the surrounding cliff face with crimson goo, and Robyn felt queasy for a moment before the blur of a bolt brought her to her senses. She watched as Wren's target crumpled first to its knees then face down, disappearing beneath the surface. Then Robyn fired her own arrow, as even more heads emerged from the lake.

Georgie continued to cough and splutter, but gradually, the coughs became less frequent and she managed to regain a little more control of her breathing. Robyn and Wren kept firing, and one by one, the beasts went down. Then…respite; a small gap where nothing emerged.

There were still creatures on the clifftop, and countless more somewhere in the lake, but for the time being, they were staying hidden.

"Come on," Robyn said, "We need to get out of here."

Wren flung her rucksack over her shoulders and ran across to help Georgie to her feet. Robyn kept her bow firmly in her right hand and bent down a little so Georgie could place an arm over her shoulder for support. The crutch was somewhere in the lake, as was Georgie's Glock 17. The surrounding landscape was barren, and the only way Georgie stood a chance was with help.

"Thank you," Georgie said weakly as she turned to look at Robyn.

"Don't thank me yet, Georgie, before today's over you might change your mind."

25

Robyn and Wren were almost running as they made their escape from the water's edge. Georgie, still dazed, managed to hop along between them keeping her sprained ankle off the ground. Robyn turned to see two more beasts were climbing to their feet. "Keep going. I'll hold them off," she said, unwrapping Georgie's arm from around her shoulder.

Robyn drew an arrow, placed it in the bow and brought the sight window up. She looked behind her to make sure Wren and Georgie were still moving, then turned back and fired, immediately drawing another arrow and firing again. A few more seconds and Georgie and her sister would be around the turn and out of sight. Another beast fell from the cliff at the far end of the lake. How long would it be before they had all fallen?

Robyn turned and began to run. Before she took the bend, she fired a glance back to the shore, but it was clear. She caught up to the others and wrapped Georgie's arm back around her shoulder. There was a long, winding track downhill; it cut through the cliffs, snaking around bends. At every turn, they expected the worst, and at every turn, Robyn and Wren turned to see if they were being followed.

The track gave way to a sprawling yard with a Portakabin at the far end, next to a chain-link fence. There was a wide gate, big enough to allow access to monstrous construction vehicles and lorries, but the rusted chains and dilapidated signage suggested this place had been abandoned long ago.

"Erm...I don't suppose anybody's got any bolt cutters," Wren asked as the three of them continued to struggle towards the exit. When they reached it, Robyn and Georgie leant up against the chain links, desperate to catch their breath while Wren frantically shook at the gate to see if there was enough give for them to sneak through, realising instantly that there was not. "Seriously? Seriously?" she said, raising her voice. She looked up to the sky. "You don't think we deserve just one break? If you want us dead so badly, why not just strike us down now? Come on! Do it!" she shouted, throwing her arms wide.

Robyn walked across to her sister and placed a gentle hand on her shoulder. "Wren...sis...it's okay."

Wren brought her eyes down to meet Robyn's, "No it isn't. Not for a second."

Georgie limped over, keeping one hand on the fence for support. "We're just going to have to climb it."

"How are you going to climb?" Wren asked. "How are we going to get over the barbed wire without being ripped to bits?"

Georgie slipped off her jacket, almost losing her balance, but being caught by Robyn just in time. "Put this over the top," she said.

Wren took a breath and started to compose herself again. She slipped her gilet off, grabbed the jacket from Georgie, and flung them both over her shoulder before making her ascent. Wren held on to the chain links tight as she draped one then the other over the barbed wire, pushing them down to see if any sharp points penetrated.

"This might work. We need to be careful, though," Wren said.

"As you're up there already, you may as well climb over first," Robyn said.

Wren looked back to the direction they had travelled from to see if any creatures had made it from the lake. The coast was clear, and she hoisted herself up, rucksack and all, flipping one leg over the side, then her other leg and finally her body, before dropping back down gracefully.

"Now you," Robyn said to Georgie.

"No, it's more important—"

"You're not going to be able to get up by yourself. Now don't argue."

Georgie looked to the top of the fence and realised Robyn was right. She gave a slight nod, then grabbed hold of the links, placing the toe of her left boot as high as she could on the fence before hoisting herself up. Her head rose above the top of the gate, and she almost forgot about her ankle and tried to move her right foot to take the next step, but suddenly remembered herself. Robyn grabbed the heel of Georgie's left foot with both her hands and pushed up hard and fast. Feeling the surge of momentum, Georgie grabbed onto the frame of the gate beneath the jacket and lifted herself, feeling her biceps strain under the weight.

"Bobbi!" Wren shouted. "They're coming."

Robyn could not turn to look without stranding Georgie on the fence. She grunted as she pushed harder, desperate to get Georgie high enough so she could make the rest of the journey to the other side under her own volition. Robyn looked towards Wren; she shook her head gently to imply there was nothing she could do. Wren flipped her rucksack off, grabbed her crossbows and loaded them. Helping Georgie would have to wait now; this was her sister.

"Forget about me," Georgie said, glancing back.

The creatures were ambling clumsily in their soaking clothes, but once they locked eyes on the three women, they suddenly began to sprint, drops of water sprayed off them as their feet pounded down the track. There were five of them, but Wren knew more would be coming. She found it difficult to aim through the fence. She sighted one and pulled the trigger, but the flight brushed against a metal link and veered off course a few metres. She fired another. The bolt flew gracefully until it landed in the stomach of one of the creatures, having no effect on its forward momentum.

"It's no good, Bobbi. I can't get them from this side."

Robyn heaved once more, grunting as she used every cell in her muscles to push Georgie to safety. Suddenly, her hands and arms moved up freely as the weight was gone. Georgie flipped her right leg over the top of the fence, quickly followed by her left. There was a shuddering clatter followed by a grunt of pain as her knees smashed the thick wire links on the other side before she dropped down. Wren caught her, but not before Georgie inadvertently put weight on her right foot. She screamed and they both went falling to the floor.

Robyn immediately swivelled around, grabbing her bow from where she had left it leaning against the fence and nocking an arrow. She fired. One of the beasts instantly dropped to the ground, but the remaining four were still charging towards her. She wasn't a freaky genius like her sister, but even she knew that there was no way out of this. As she nocked another arrow, she realised even if she dropped her bow and tried to scramble up the gate she would not have enough time. She wanted to close her eyes, wish it all away, but she was not that girl anymore.

She fired again. The centre creature dropped to the ground, but the other three kept coming, bunching in now like an arrowhead. She heard a grunt and a yelp of pain from behind her, or was it a cry of pity? A cry of regret, as saving Georgie had now cost Robyn her life? She fired again—the last shot she would get off before they were on her. There was a blur as two small missiles appeared from above. The bolts smashed through the skulls of the middle and right-hand beast. The middle creature was the one Robyn's arrow sank into as well.

She immediately realised what had happened, dropped her bow to the ground and kicked out as hard as she could. Her foot sank into the last creature's stomach; there was a spray of water as its soaked clothing stretched and wrung beneath her boot. It flew backwards and Robyn grabbed an arrow from one of her quivers. She leapt on top of the beast, almost at the same time as it crashed to the ground. Its hands reflexively reached towards her, but Robyn plunged the arrow through its eye, rendering it lifeless...more lifeless.

Robyn's chest heaved in and out as she tried to bring her breathing back under control. She turned back towards the fence and saw Wren, both arms over the top of the gate, the crossbows still aiming towards the creatures. Beneath her, Georgie had a look of agony on her face as she continued to support Wren's weight on her shoulders while clutching onto the fence for all she was worth.

"Come on, Bobbi," Wren said, "there are more coming." Robyn turned to look up the track to see further creatures heading down towards them. She climbed to her feet, passed the bow and quivers underneath the narrow gap at the bottom of the gate and took a firm grip of the fence. Wren jumped back down, and Georgie slumped to the floor, cradling her ankle.

Robyn levered herself up over the top, carefully peeled the two jackets from the barbed wire, and then jumped down to the other side. She put the quivers and bow over her shoulder then both sisters helped Georgie back to her feet before they continued their journey. They were just a few feet away from the fence when there was an almighty crash as six beasts threw themselves at the chained barrier.

Robyn and Wren both looked back, just an extra precaution to make sure that, by some miracle, they had not managed to smash through. They looked beyond the snarling faces further up the track to see even more monsters emerging from around the bend.

Robyn, Wren and Georgie continued until the sandy track met the road. "Which way now?" Robyn asked.

"Right...we turn right," Georgie replied. It was a country lane lined with trees on either side

"We need to find somewhere to rest," Wren said. "We need to get off the road. While ever that fire's burning, we run the risk of a horde of those things getting us."

The three of them carried on. The going was slow and every rustle from the trees put them on high alert. They'd been walking for over fifteen minutes when Georgie spotted something, "Over there," she said.

"What?" the sister's asked at the same time, worried they were about to be attacked.

"A house," she replied. Georgie was looking across a field through a small gap in the trees.

"That'll do," Robyn replied.

"Hang on, Bobbi, we don't know anything about it. It could be—"

"What's there to know? We need shelter, there's nowhere else."

"She's got a point," Georgie said. "I want to get back home more than anything, but it's just a matter of time until we run into those things and I don't know how many more lucky escapes we've got in us. I'm doing nothing but holding you back."

They climbed over the stone wall bordering the field and began their trek to the farmhouse. They ducked down in the tall grass as they got nearer before stopping completely. There was no sign of danger, but that meant little these days.

"Stay here," Wren said, "I'll go check it out."

"No, I'll check it out," Robyn replied, standing up. "I might not be as fast as you, but I can reload quicker." Before Wren had the chance to argue, Robyn was running towards the farmyard.

"Oh god, Bobbi, please be careful," Wren said softly as her sister disappeared.

A few minutes passed and Wren became increasingly concerned. "Don't worry; she's a smart girl," Georgie said, sensing her tension.

"It's just—"

"There! She's there," Georgie replied.

Robyn appeared from the other side of the house. She ran back across, not bothering to stay low this time. "It's all clear. Bit of a dump, looks like the Loch Uig crowd have already paid this place a visit, but if anything, that should make it safer."

"You were a long time, we were worried," Wren said.

"Yeah well, I wanted to check the place out properly," she replied, helping Georgie to her feet. The three of them struggled across to the farmhouse, the events of the day now beginning to weigh them down. They piled in through the door, closing it firmly behind them. The kitchen cupboards were all open and empty. Three of the chairs had toppled over, and as the women made their way into the living room, they saw that similar mayhem had ensued in there. Pictures hung lopsided on the wall. Big chunks of plaster were missing where furniture had been removed. The fireplace tool set had been toppled spreading soot all over the beige rug. The curtains were still hanging and an old, but comfortable-looking couch sat against one wall.

"Let's get you settled," Wren said, guiding Georgie to the sofa.

"Wait a minute. I'm soaked. We're all going to catch our death of cold if we don't get out of these clothes."

"I'll go and see if there are any clothes," Wren said, disappearing out of the small living room.

"You okay, Georgie?" Robyn asked.

"No. I feel…"

"What is it?"

"I should be trying to get home, to warn them to get out, but right now, I know it's way too dangerous out there. I feel stuck between a rock and a hard place."

"Look, we'll stop here tonight then look at getting out tomorrow. We can't be that far from the Manor. It's not like it won't take that mob time to reboot. They got their arses handed to them today."

"I suppose you're right."

Wren walked back into the room carrying a bin bag full of stuff, with a big smile on her face. I found a load of clothes, curtains and towels in a built-in wardrobe in one of the bedrooms. It looked like an old lady's room…smelt like one too, so I'm guessing they weren't too interested in the contents."

"Why are you smiling?" Robyn asked.

"Looks like Grandma was a secret boozer," she said, pulling a three-quarter full bottle of whisky from the bag.

"Score," Robyn said.

"Yeah, I'll take that," Georgie said grabbing the bottle. "Both of you are too young to drink."

Robyn grabbed it back, "We both aged ten years today carrying your crippled arse everywhere so this bottle shares three ways."

They all laughed until a more serious look came over Georgie's face. "Girls…I just want to say…"

"No need. You'd have done the same for us," Wren replied.

"Yeah but…"

"No need," Robyn said.

"Okay, before I get out of these clothes, I want to block these windows out properly. The second it gets dark we can start a fire and get our clothes dry," Wren said.

"I'll give you a hand," Robyn said.

"I'll—" Georgie began.

"You'll get weight off that ankle," Wren interrupted.

"Yes, Mum."

"Here," Wren said, handing her the bin bag.

"Where did you get the bin bag from?"

"It was on the top shelf of the wardrobe. There were a load of photo albums in it," Wren replied sadly.

"I see," Georgie said.

Robyn and Wren got to work. They headed outside and into the barn. It had been ransacked, like the rest of the house, but over in one corner stood five internal doors. It looked like they had been a project at some stage. They had been stripped of paint and partially sanded, but now the accumulation of dust suggested they had been long forgotten.

"Those," Wren said pointing.

"What about them?" Robyn asked.

"They'll be great for helping to block out the light."

Robyn walked over to them and tried to lift one. "Are you sure you can't find something heavier? A wall, maybe?"

"Stop being a wimp," Wren said, smiling and angling the door towards her.

Half an hour later, the only light coming into the living room was through the open door leading from the kitchen diner. The dining chairs had been set up around the fire, ready for night to fall. They had broken the dining table and one of the chairs up for firewood and had carefully laid their soaking garments out, ready for drying. The choice of clothes in the bag had been depressingly old fashioned, and all had a foisty smell, but at least the bath towels smelled freshly washed. Georgie, Robyn and Wren all sat on the couch looking like they had just stepped out of the shower at a football match. They were exhausted, a little bewildered, and now they felt like they were in limbo, just waiting for night to come.

"I'm starving," Robyn said.

Wren stood and went across to her rucksack, which was laid on the floor in front of the fireplace. She reached in and brought out four granola bars. She handed one each to the girls, kept one for herself, and placed the other on the mantlepiece. "We'll save that for breakfast." She walked back to sit on the sofa and the three of them peeled off the plastic wrappers and began to savour the crunchy snack bars.

Wren sneezed. "We'll be lucky if we don't get pneumonia after today," she said.

"Don't worry, sis," Robyn said, rubbing her towel-covered back gently. "Pneumonia takes a while to set in. We'll have been eaten by a pack of hungry zombies way before then."

The words hung in the air for a moment before they all burst out laughing. They laughed and laughed, much more than the joke deserved. Wren accidentally broke wind. "Oops, 'scuse me," she said, putting three fingers up to her mouth and making them all laugh even more.

"I think you're covering up the wrong end there, sis," Robyn said.

"Okay, who's for a jolt?" Georgie asked, putting her granola bar down and reaching for the bottle.

"Hang on," Wren said, climbing to her feet. "We need glasses." She went into the kitchen, returning a moment later with three tumblers. She sat back down, and Georgie poured them all a double measure, only then looking at the bottle.

"Granny was a connoisseur; this is the good stuff," she said, placing the top back on and holding her glass up.

"To the two bravest girls I've ever met," she said.

Robyn and Wren suddenly looked embarrassed. Robyn lifted her glass. "To friends."

All three of them clinked glasses and repeated, "To friends," before each taking a drink.

Wren winced as the whisky burnt her throat, but then she raised her glass once more. "To lost friends."

There was a pause this time, as the events of the day caught up with them. So much had happened in such a short time. Tomorrow they were going to head back to the Manor to evacuate, get the hell out of there as fast as they could, leaving all their plans, all their hopes behind.

Today had been a long, painful day. They had lost people. And deep inside, they knew it was only the beginning. There would be many painful days and a lot more losses ahead.

"To lost friends," they said, clinking their glasses once more time.

26

Their stomachs rumbled as they finished the granola bars. Wren went back to search the kitchen, but there was not a grain of food in the house. She returned to the living room, plonking herself back down on the sofa. "I don't think we'll get much sleep with our growling bellies tonight," she said.

"Don't worry about that," Georgie replied, "A few glasses of this stuff and we'll pass out until morning."

"Should we really be drinking it then? Shouldn't we have our wits about us?" Wren asked.

"I don't know about you, but I don't have another fight or another run left in me today. If someone or something comes in the night, I want to be so tanked, I don't even notice," Georgie replied.

"You make a good point," Robyn said, gulping the remainder of the amber liquid in her glass before lifting it for a refill.

Not wanting to feel left out, Wren did the same, immediately feeling the effect of the whisky as it went to her head. She sneezed again, "Oh god, I'm definitely getting a cold," she said.

The three of them sat there, occasionally having their glasses refilled until they started to feel a comforting fogginess taking the edge off.

"Screw this, I'm starting the fire," Robyn said.

"Blobbi, no it's not light yet."

Robyn and Georgie both burst out laughing. "Erm…sis, maybe you should go easy on the hooch."

"What? Why's wrong?"

"Just slow down a little," Robyn said, standing up and walking to the doorway. Night was starting to close in. By the time the fire had taken and it was throwing out any significant amount of smoke, it would be dark. Robyn closed the door, firmly rendering the room black. They had carefully plugged all the gaps with curtains, clothes— anything they could find, and now no light could get in or out. She carefully felt her way to the fireplace, then fumbled for the lighter. "God, I hope this still works," she said, flicking the wheel to get a flame.

"Don't worry," Georgie replied, I know how to start a fire if it doesn't."

The flame caught and Robyn ignited the paper and kindling in the fireplace. It slowly began to catch and start burning. The flames grew higher and when she was happy the fire would not extinguish, she stood up and turned around.

Georgie started laughing. "Just what did you have in mind tonight?"

"Huh? I don't get you," Robyn said, looking at Wren, who had fallen to one side in hysterics.

Georgie couldn't speak either now and just pointed towards Robyn. Wren broke wind again. "Oops," she managed to say in between fits of laughter.

Robyn looked behind her, then she looked down. "Oh my god," she said, suddenly realising she was naked. She looked across to the door to see the corner of the towel stuck between it and the jamb. Her senses had clearly been more than a little dimmed by the alcohol, as up until this very second, she had not even noticed it had come off. She ran over to the door, opened it slightly, grabbed the towel, and wrapped it around before going back to sit on the sofa. "That's so embarrassing," she said, taking another drink.

Eventually, the laughter of the other two slowed then died. "Just be grateful it was just us two," Georgie said, giggling a little once again.

"I suppose," Robyn said, taking another drink. "It's good stuff this, though," she said, raising the glass.

"You're not kidding. Not only can I not feel my ankle anymore, I can't feel my legs," Georgie said.

The three of them continued to drink and watch the flames dance in the fireplace, until one by one they drifted off to sleep.

The next morning, Wren woke up on the rug in front of the fire. The last thing she remembered doing was turning the drying clothes around on the chairs, and she had not made it back to the couch; she had just curled up on the floor. Her mouth felt about the same as the rough fabric she was lying on, and her head had an aching fuzziness that threatened worse to come. She looked at her watch. "Oh my god," she said, suddenly springing up. The room was dark but for the glow of the embers, and she headed to the door to let in more light.

Robyn's head was on one arm of the sofa, Georgie's was on the other, and even the noise of the door opening and the influx of light had not woken them.

Wren walked back across to the chairs and felt her clothes. They were bone dry now, like her mouth and throat. She reached into her rucksack and pulled out the bottle of water. She took a few sips before replacing the lid. This was all they had until they could find a fresh supply. She began to put on her clothes.

"Ugh...What time is it?" Georgie asked, slowly rising from her slumber.

"Eleven."

"Eleven?" she replied.

"My head," Robyn said, not moving her body, but slowly flicking her eyes open.

Georgie swung her feet onto the floor and flinched as she tried to put even the smallest amount of pressure on.

"No better?" Wren asked.

"Worse, actually," Georgie replied.

Suddenly, Wren's head was not as fuzzy anymore. She understood immediately what that meant.

"Okay, you're going to have to stay here."

"What?" Georgie asked, her grogginess vanishing just as quickly.

"Look, it makes sense. No offence, but if we get into another tight spot out there…" Wren trailed off, letting Georgie fill in the blanks for herself.

Robyn leaned herself up too, now. Her eyes were just slits for the time being, but she was looking towards her sister. "What are you saying?"

"I doubt if we're more than three, four miles tops away from the Manor. I could make it there pretty quickly by myself. I could tell people what's happened...that we need to pack up and get the hell out. Then, while all that's in motion, come back here in a vehicle and get you two."

"Okay, I understand me not going, but why won't you and Robyn go together? It's dangerous out there for anybody, but a young girl by herself...if you get hurt," Georgie said gesturing down to her ankle, "It would be all over."

"What happens if this place gets attacked? You'd be here by yourself."

"This place has already been attacked, Wren. They're not going to come back for some old lady's clothing and a few towels," Georgie replied.

"Georgie's right," Robyn said, swinging her legs off the couch and walking over to the chair with her clothes on. "I'm going with you."

Ten minutes later, Robyn and Wren were out of the house, running cross-country. The distant black smoke was not rising in plumes anymore, but as one giant cloud. They kept close to walls and fences, gaining as much cover as they could. Only once did they see a zombie. It had suffered some kind of disablement, and its leg jutted out at an unnatural angle. That did not halt its resolve, though. It was no threat to them as it continued to make its way towards the rising blackness of the forest.

They left the fields, entering more woodland, and finally, Wren came to a stop. "Hang on, I recognise this," she said.

"I don't."

"You surprise me."

"Woods is woods. What is there to recognise?"

"That tree over there. We were out here the other day. That's where we found all those oyster mushrooms," she said, running up to it and rubbing a gentle hand over the surface.

"Ughhh! You're such a dork!" Robyn said, walking across to her.

"This is good. It means we're not far away," Wren said, standing up again and beginning to head in a different direction.

"If you say so," Robyn said, turning a full three-hundred and sixty degrees before continuing after her sister.

They walked just two more minutes and came to a stop once again. Now Robyn did recognise where they were. They were on the south side of the valley, and diagonally across from them stood the familiar white wall of the Manor. The valley was silent as the black smoke continued to bellow a few miles away. Robyn and Wren continued along the tree line, cautiously surveying the area, making sure there were no lurking surprises.

They stopped when they were in line with the bridge at the bottom and then finally broke their cover, sprinting down the hill before scrambling back up as quickly as they could. They reached the wall on the other side and turned, dreading what they would see. They travelled all this way from the farmhouse and had not broken cover once, but in this last strait, they had, and they were only too aware of what danger that incurred. Robyn half-raised her hand to reach for an arrow before stopping.

"Huh!" Wren said. "It's our lucky day."

The sisters followed the wall around until Robyn stopped again. "Do you hear that?" she asked.

"I don't hear anything," Wren replied.

"Exactly."

Wren had one of her pistol crossbows in her hand, already loaded. She had set off like that from the farmhouse and had anticipated needing it several times before reaching the sanctuary of the Manor. But now, it seemed like the very place where she had sought safety was going to be the place where she needed her bow the most.

Robyn grabbed an arrow and raised her bow then the two of them continued, more slowly now. They followed the wall around and ducked down, looking in the direction of the entrance. From their angle, they could not see the giant gates, so Wren slowly edged to her left, staying low behind the shrubbery.

Robyn looked towards her. "It's open," Wren mouthed, giving a gesture with her hand. The two sisters stayed perfectly still, but nothing came in or out of the gates and the silence continued to stiffen the air around them.

Wren began to creep forwards, and Robyn immediately pulled back the bowstring, ready for anything. Wren angled her head as she approached the entrance. She stood slowly and walked to the midpoint of where the two gates normally met. Her mouth dropped open a little, but no other movement was forthcoming.

"Wren?" Robyn hissed, "Wren?" she said louder, eventually standing up to join her. Before she even got there, she could see that a huge hole had been smashed through the left-hand gate. The hinges clung on to a few wooden fragments, but that was all. She stood by her sister's side, her mouth dropped open, too.

Neither of them knew how long they'd stood there, but it was more than seconds and more than just a couple of minutes. Their eyes took in everything; an entire landscape of horror lay before them.

Dozens of bodies lay still and bloody on the ground—men, women and children. The two sisters slowly walked through the gaping entrance. Robyn dropped to her knees. She laid down her bow and placed a gentle hand on Pippa's cold forehead. Patricia's arm was still wrapped around her. By their side lay Steven, and a few feet away was Dan. His eyes were still open, but the paleness of his skin told Robyn that his final breath had been some time since. Robert and Amelia were still holding hands, even in death.

Wren knelt down beside her sister and wove her right hand into Robyn's left. Then it left them; the control they had tried so hard to maintain, the composure they had drawn on in so many situations. It started as a single tear, a single shuddering breath, a single sob. Wren reached out and took Pippa's tiny, cold hand. There was a sticky residue on it–honey, and that made Wren cry even harder. She was just a little girl; a sweet little girl with dolls and a land of make-believe in her head and sticky, sticky hands. She looked across towards Robert and Amelia and now her sobbing turned into baying cries. She let go of Pippa and placed her arms around Robyn as the two of them knelt there amid all the carnage, unable to believe what evil thrived in the hearts of some men.

"They were looking for you," said a voice.

Robyn and Wren broke their clutch, and despite the heartache they were feeling, grabbed their weapons and sprang to their feet, turning sharply. They relaxed again as they saw Susan standing there. The tears still stung their eyes and they were not finished crying or mourning, but the surprise of finding someone alive gave them a moment's respite from the aching sadness.

"How do you know?" Wren asked, her voice shivering.

"I saw and heard everything that went on," she replied.

"How?"

Susan pointed to a tiny window above the second floor in the Manor. "The attic. That was my safe place when I was young. I live there now."

Robyn and Wren gave each other a puzzled look. "Are you okay?" Robyn asked, her voice quivering, just like her sister's.

"I'm fine. Why do you ask?"

"This…?" Robyn replied, gesturing around her.

"How do you know they were looking for us? And where's everybody else?" Wren asked.

A distant smile crept across Susan's face. "When you didn't return yesterday…when everybody saw the smoke…a lot of them took their vehicles and went." Susan looked at the people lying dead on the ground. "These were the ones who had faith in you and the others, the ones who felt sure you'd return." The smile on her face broadened for a second, but then disappeared again.

"And they just massacred them?" Robyn asked.

"No…not at first. There was one man. He asked about you by name. He described you down to your pretty blue eyes," she said, looking towards Wren. "He was convinced you were hiding out here somewhere. So…he started killing people one by one until someone told him where you were. He had a firing squad lined up, and he walked up and down the rows telling them they'd be spared if they gave you up. People kept saying. We don't know…they never came back, but that just made him madder. Then…he marched to the front and just nodded and that was it. The gunfire didn't ring out for long, and when it was over, he pulled a gun from his waistband and just started shooting them. Even though they were already dead, he started shooting and he didn't stop until his gun was empty."

"Oh my god," Robyn said.

"They came here with a convoy of vehicles. They emptied the cellars in no time. They took the remainder of the vehicles that were left here too. Then they disappeared as fast as they'd arrived. I don't think I've ever seen anybody as angry as that man was."

Robyn and Wren just stood there, looking at the bodies, imagining how it had all happened. Wren finally broke her gaze and looked towards Susan once again. "You should come with us," she said, with tears still streaming from her eyes.

"Why would I do that?" she asked, a lopsided smile still hanging on her face. "This is my home."

"But...there's nothing left," Wren replied.

"What do you mean?" she said, holding her arms out and twirling around. "I've got the whole place to myself now."

"Susan, I think you should come with us. You're not really thinking straight right now," Robyn said.

Susan smiled. "No...I'm happy. For the first time in a long time, I'm happy."

Wren and Robyn looked towards each other once again. "Susan, Wren and me would really like you to—"

"Don't you see? It was a sign. They tore the place apart looking for you, but they didn't find me. That secret attic was always my special place," she said, smiling again.

"If you stay, what will you eat?" Wren asked distantly.

"I've got some things up there and they didn't take anything from the servants' quarters. There's food in their cupboards, too, and then I've got those," she said, pointing over to the polytunnels.

"They didn't take all the food?" Wren asked, slowly heading towards the steps. Robyn followed her, leaving Susan alone.

"She's gone well and truly," Robyn said as they both walked through the entrance. The place looked different now. Granted, their tear glazed eyes made it hard to focus, but the Manor somehow looked like a shadowy replica of itself, like its grand life, its history had been erased, and all that stood in its place was a hollowed-out shell.

"We can't force her to come with us," Wren said as they continued down the hallway towards the servants' apartments. On reaching them, they saw the doors had been kicked in, but on entering their flat, they saw nothing had been taken.

"I don't understand. Why wouldn't they take everything like they did back at the farm? It's weird," Robyn said, wiping her eyes.

"Weird nothing. They're coming back here. Nobody leaves food." Wren ran into the bathroom and grabbed a thick, luxurious towel before heading back to the kitchen and laying it out on the counter. She took her rucksack off and handed it to Robyn. Head into Georgie's place and pack all the food and water you can find," Wren said, sniffing hard and wiping her nose on the back of her hand. Robyn took the rucksack and disappeared while Wren began to place tins, packets, and bottles of water into the centre of the towel. When the cupboards and fridge were empty, she scrunched it up like a giant bindle and heaved it over her shoulder before picking up her bow in her right hand and going to look for Robyn.

"I found a holdall," Robyn said. I've packed a few bits of clothing for Georgie and some photos. I'm going to put some stuff in for us, then we need to get out of here." She paused. "Are you sure they'll be back?"

"They probably didn't expect to find all they did. I mean, the generators, the tools, this is a lot of stuff to shift. Remember how they gutted the farm? They'll do the same here. Now come on," Wren said.

They were back outside within five minutes to find Susan still standing there among the bodies, like she was standing in the middle of a field of poppies. She still had a slight smile on her face, until she cast eyes on the two sisters once more.

"Listen, Susan—" Robyn started.

"Go!" Susan hissed. The calmness from a few minutes before was gone now. "Go and leave me alone. None of this would have happened if it wasn't for you two. I brought you here, to my home, and this is the price I've paid. This is the price my parents paid. I hate you. I hate both of you. Just go!" Her eyes looked wild, and her lips peeled back in an animalistic snarl, then she turned around and walked back into the house. Robyn was about to go after her, but Wren put a hand out to stop her.

"It's too late for her," Wren said as tears began to roll down her face again. "We need to go."

"She's right, though. This is because of us." Robyn said, looking around at all the bodies again.

"I know," Wren replied.

*

The journey back to the house was a slow one by design. Neither of them wanted to be the ones to break the news to Georgie that her daughter and parents were dead. The black smoke still billowed into the sky, and the smell of fire prickled in their noses even from several miles away. They took breaks often as the weight of what they were carrying required far more exertion from the pair of them.

The two hardly spoke, both lost in the same thoughts, the same sadness, the same guilt. They saw the faces of the dead one after the other like a morbid sideshow. Then Robyn suddenly remembered her idea, the Day of the Dead, and she broke down. They both sat for a while on a black stone wall, gripping onto each other like they were the only ones left in the world. Neither could remember a time when they had cried more, when they had felt so lost. Eventually, they broke their grasp, climbed off the wall, continued their journey.

They finally reached the farm, making their way across the field to the house. When they walked through the door, Georgie was sat on a kitchen work surface. The bottle of whisky was by her side, almost empty. Her eyes were red and tears streaked her face. Wren hoisted the bindle over her shoulder and onto the floor, placing the bow down on another countertop.

"They're gone, aren't they?" Georgie said, her eyes knowing the answer, but the tiniest glint of hope remained.

Wren gulped and tears began to run down her cheeks again. All she could do was nod.

Robyn dragged the rucksack from her shoulders and placed it down. She reached into a side pocket and pulled out a handful of photographs. "I'm sorry," she said, passing them to Georgie. "I'm sorry…I'm so sorry." She threw her arms around the grieving mother and they held each other tightly.

"I'm so sorry, Georgie," Wren said, moving her own arms around the pair of them. They stayed there, holding onto each other, crying, baying with the pain. The minutes passed by, and they eventually released each other. They took deep, trembling breaths and shared pained looks. They remained silent but for their quivering breathing until Georgie finally spoke.

"Promise me something," she said, reaching out for Wren's hand.

Wren looked through Georgie's blurry, tearful eyes and into her very soul. "Anything," she replied.

"Promise me we'll make them pay for this."

Wren stared hard at Georgie, and then squeezed her hand even tighter. "I promise you."

The End

A NOTE FROM THE AUTHOR

I really hope you enjoyed this book and would be very grateful if you took a minute to leave a review on Amazon and Goodreads.

If you would like to stay informed about what I'm doing, including current writing projects, and all the latest news and release information; these are the places to go:

Join the fan club on Facebook
https://www.facebook.com/groups/127693634504226

Like the Christopher Artinian author page
https://www.facebook.com/safehaventrilogy/

Buy exclusive and signed books and merchandise, subscribe to the newsletter and follow the blog:
https://www.christopherartinian.com/

Follow me on Twitter
https://twitter.com/Christo71635959

Follow me on Amazon
https://amzn.to/2I1llU6

Follow me on Goodreads
https://bit.ly/2P7iDzX

Other books by Christopher Artinian:

Safe Haven: Rise of the RAMs
Safe Haven: Realm of the Raiders
Safe Haven: Reap of the Righteous
Safe Haven: Ice
Before Safe Haven: Lucy
Before Safe Haven: Alex
Before Safe Haven: Mike
The End of Everything: Book 1
The End of Everything: Book 2
The End of Everything: Book 3
The End of Everything: Book 4

Anthologies featuring short stories by Christopher
Artinian

Undead Worlds: A Reanimated Writers Anthology

Featuring: Before Safe Haven: Losing the Battle by Christopher Artinian

Tales from Zombie Road: The Long-Haul Anthology

Featuring: Condemned by Christopher Artinian

Treasured Chests: A Zombie Anthology for Breast Cancer Care

Featuring: Last Light by Christopher Artinian

Trick or Treat Thrillers (Best Paranormal 2018) Featuring: The Akkadian Vessel.

CHRISTOPHER ARTINIAN

Christopher Artinian was born and raised in Leeds, West Yorkshire. Wanting to escape life in a big city and concentrate more on working to live than living to work, he and his family moved to the Outer Hebrides in the north-west of Scotland in 2004, where he now works as a full-time author.

Chris is a huge music fan, a cinephile, an avid reader and a supporter of Yorkshire county cricket club. When he's not sat in front of his laptop living out his next post-apocalyptic/dystopian/horror adventure, he will be passionately immersed in one of his other interests.

Printed in Great Britain
by Amazon